Looker

Also by Stanley Bennett Clay

In Search of Pretty Young Black Men

Diva

Looker

A Novel

STANLEY BENNETT CLAY

ATRIA BOOKS

New York   London   Toronto   Sydney

ATRIA BOOKS
1230 Avenue of the Americas
New York, NY 10020

"To Have Loved," composed by Stanley Bennett Clay; © 2007
by Clatonian Sound Music

Library of Congress Cataloging-in-Publication Data

Clay, Stanley.
    Looker : a novel / Stanley Bennett Clay.—1st Atria Books paperback ed.
      p. cm.
     1. African American men—Fiction. 2. Gay men—Fiction. I. Title.
    PS3603.L39L66 2007
     813'.6—dc22   2007060652

ISBN-13: 978-0-7432-9102-6
ISBN-10:   0-7432-9102-6

First Atria Books paperback edition June 2007

10 9 8 7 6 5 4 3 2 1

ATRIA BOOKS is a trademark of Simon & Schuster, Inc.

Manufactured in the United States of America

For information about special discounts for bulk purchases,
please contact Simon & Schuster Special Sales at
1-800-456-6798 or business@simonandschuster.com.

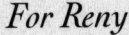

For Reny

God is love . . . and love is for everyone.
—BISHOP CARL BEAN

Prologue

He remembered the last time he saw Grammy alive. June 23, 1983. It was the day of his high school graduation. The moment the police found him on campus, he tore out of his cap and gown and rushed with them to the hospital.

"You want me to come along with you?" Brando caught up with him, grabbing his arm.

"Nah, man, stay. Graduate. I'll handle it."

He found himself praying so hard that the tears streamed down his face. The screaming police siren thankfully drowned out what was the beginning of sobs. But he knew he would have to stop. He knew he couldn't let Grammy see him like this, crying and dripping and blaming himself, knowing that she had been headed to Hamilton High School, to see her only grandchild graduate with honors, when the accident happened.

In spite of the tubes in her arm and nostrils, she seemed ever so peaceful laid out in that hospital bed.

The doctor desperately pleaded with his mother, Betty Stevens, Grammy's daughter. Johnnie Mae Stevens had lost too much blood and desperately needed a transfusion, but Sister Betty would not budge. It was simply a matter of conscience, a test of unshakable faith.

"It is against Jehovah's will to take blood in our system," she responded with evangelical pride.

"Talk to your mother, son. You have to convince her," the doctor had said. "It's the only chance your grandmother has."

And so for the first time in three years he talked to his mother; pleaded with her, begged her, set aside what had divided and wounded them.

In his mother's eyes he would always be her forgotten sin, a saintly reminder of one evil night eighteen years earlier, when she writhed and sweated, fornicated with so many boys that she did not even know who the coculprit was who caused her to bring a bastard child into the world.

Never again, I am Jesus' now.

She took the pain of the birth as penance for being vile and welcomed the punishment of labor like the lash.

Never again, I am Jesus' now.

She forgot about Willie and Jerome and what's-his-name with the really big one, and Sonny, who took her from behind.

"Sin begets sin," she preached to her bastard over and over and over again. She beat him with razor straps when she mistook wonder for wanton desires rising up in his little-boy eyes.

She threw him out of her Jehovah-blessed house when, at fourteen, he sinned against nature and performed sinful, unnatural acts with another sinful, unnatural boy.

"Sin begets sin," she preached and she preached.

Grammy tried hard not to spoil him, but it was simply

2

beyond her control. Her only grandchild had been through enough. So it was not a spoiling, it was merely giving him what he had not gotten elsewhere. Grammy took him in, much to the chagrin of her sanctified daughter, his mother, and reared him into young manhood.

And now Grammy was dying. So he broke down and spoke to his mother for the first time in three years, pleaded with her to let the doctor save Grammy. But it was as if he did not even exist, save for the sinful stench Sister Betty believed she smelled.

He stayed long into the night at the hospital. When the doctor finally pronounced Grammy dead, his mother prayed silently and ignored his cursing and crying.

That night, his best friend, Brando, came over to the house Omar had shared with his Grammy. Omar tried so hard to be strong, but Brando knew better. Omar cried in Brando's arms until morning.

That was more than twenty years ago. Omar still cries on occasion, when he thinks about June 23, 1983, when he thinks about Grammy. And Brando is still his best friend.

Part One

Chapter One

Brando Heywood woke up at his usual Sunday-morning time, 6:30 AM. Enough time to climb out of bed, put on the coffee, grab the paper off the front porch, read and browse the book review, opinion, calendar, hot properties, sports, and travel sections. He had plenty of time to clean himself up and meet his parents for First Sunday's second service. Later he would meet Omar, who Brando couldn't drag inside a church if his life depended on it. But Brando understood.

Brando Heywood was a nice guy with a good heart. He was a tight 170 pounds hung on a well-toned five-eleven frame. His handsome face sported a distant but cordial smile and dark cocoa doe eyes almost as dark as his smooth jet skin.

He had been well liked all throughout adolescence and puberty, excelled as everyone had expected in middle and high school, graduated from Howard U and Stanford Law with obligatory honors, and was prosperous and well established as an entertainment lawyer. He had just turned forty and still looked like a student. He was modest and pleasant and never shouted in church.

But romantically, he was alone. That feeling he had known

with Collier was missing. He and Collier had been together five years before their commitment ceremony, and stayed together five years after. Brando considered the breakup amicable, the reasons arbitrary, and the blame shared graciously. They were the couple that everyone knew would last forever, yet no one was surprised when they broke up.

They were a polite and gentlemanly pair. No infidelity and, near the end, little passion. They truly loved each other, but over the years they had become too comfortable with each other. The edge that might have ignited some fire had been smoothed over like stones eternally caressed and ultimately subdued by the waters of a gently babbling brook.

The breakup simply happened. One night while they sat in front of the TV eating Pizza Hut pizza, they almost said it simultaneously: "Maybe we should break up." The slipped utterance, echoed, stopped them both cold. They looked at each other, smiled at each other, then laughed. The relief followed by this statement was filled with the first real passion they had shared in a very long time, and they knew it. The sex they had that night was their best and their last.

That was two years ago. Brando had been celibate ever since.

He now stepped out of bed and stretched his smooth naked body toward the warm Santa Ana breeze that entered through the sliding glass door of his bedroom terrace. His morning hard-on, unconsciously, freely, aimed itself at the Hollywood sign in the facing hills across the desert-lush L.A. basin.

The sun seemed brighter this Sunday morning than on any Sunday morning of his recent memory. It was winter in L.A. The warm Santa Anas blew the sky dirt-free and smogless. In spite of the smell of smoke in the air, the beauty of the sight was near religious, causing his penis to respectfully calm down to its flaccid eight inches.

He slipped on soft cotton boxers and cashmere slippers, then stepped outside for the paper. His neighbor Selma Fant, the councilman's wife, was defiantly sunning herself in the front yard next door. She peeked above her sunglasses and savored an eyeful of fine chocolate legs and well-defined torso. Then she smiled.

"Fires in Malibu again."

"I heard."

He bent down for the paper and without much thought gave her the show she had come to expect almost every Sunday morning.

Back inside Brando did his stretches in the bright wood-paneled den while Tim Russert and a team of political pundits assessed the state of the world on NBC. The sound of birds chirping and the scent of gardenias that grew wild along the slope that bordered his lap pool floated harmoniously through the opened windows of his dining room atrium, past the sunken living room, and delivered sweet scent and sound to the master of the house. On the floor he sat closed-eyed and yogalike while muted pundits debated on-screen.

The stretches felt marvelous, the bath even better. He was happy with his life. No. Satisfied. Resigned. Perhaps too resigned. The thought made him pause, then the thought disappeared.

He picked up his phone and dialed.

"Hello?" Jeanette Bell answered on the second ring.

Jeanette Bell was Pulitzer Prize–winning novelist Clymenthia Teager's manager and life partner. Her striking good looks, flawless dark olive complexion, and shapely physique kept platinum-selling rappers desperate to have her hoochie-mama in their videos. Modeling agencies offered her lucrative contracts and film people knocked at her door often. But Jeanette Bell would have none of that. That was not what she had gotten her master's in business from Carnegie Mellon for. Her looks were often a distraction and a nuisance. So many men aggressively and dangerously hit on her that Clymenthia convinced her to carry both mace and a gun.

Jeanette Bell was twenty-seven, ten years Clymenthia Teager's junior. But she equaled the noted writer, if not in literary talent and life experience, in intellect and articulation. It was Jeanette Bell who had handpicked her good friend Brando Heywood to negotiate Clymenthia's new deal with Simon & Schuster.

Jeanette was also well aware of the importance of L.A. It would get Clymenthia in with the industry crowd while keeping the East Coast black literary intelligentsia, territorial and jealous, unsuspicious of her loyalty. Tonight's signing at Eso Won Books would be a major affair.

"Morning, sunshine," Brando said with a smile in his voice.

"Hey, Bran. How's my boy?"

"Up and at 'em. What are you ladies up to this morning?"

"Getting ready for church."

"Me too. Unity Fellowship?"

"Yep. You should join us."

"And miss First Sunday on the home front? Dad would kill me."

"Clymenthia's in the shower. You need to talk to her?"

"Nah, just checking up. All set for tonight?"

"All set."

"You guys know how to get to Eso Won, right?"

"Does a bear know how to get to honey?"

"All right." He laughed.

"Brando?"

"Yeah?"

"Thanks again."

"For what?"

"The new book deal. Very nice, mister."

"Thanks," he said. "Wait until you see what we're getting for the film rights."

"Genius."

"Lucky in law, unlucky in love." He laughed again.

"You said it, not me," she warned slyly.

And he got it. "See you guys down there."

He hung up the phone, checked his watch, picked up his Bible, and then inspected himself in the hall mirror. Every hair was in place and the suit hung just right.

Selma Fant, the councilman's wife, was still sunning herself when he pulled his Mercedes out of the garage. The convertable top came down to her flirtatious smile and the want in her eyes. Councilman Felton G. Fant knew of his wife's Stella-esque fantasies. He was amused by them, pretty much assured that she was of no sexual interest to their openly gay friend next door.

"Well, don't we look nice?" the fifty-nine-year-old matron fished. She eased herself up from the chaise with a Toni Braxton slow stir and sauntered over to the driver's side of the idling convertible. She peeked seductively over her Donna Karans and displayed ample cleavage, courtesy of a skimpy two-piece swim ensemble and an expensive Sherman Oaks surgeon handy with a laser.

"Nah, you're the one." He smiled.

Without shame she stared down at the bulge between his legs.

"Nice tie," she addressed it.

"Selma, Miss Selma, Miss Fant." He laughed. "Today's Sunday, remember? The Lord's day?"

"And I'm sure the Lord won't mind a little love spreading." She then chortled back in that way of hers that let Brando know she had already had her Sunday-morning cocktail.

"I'm going to see Miss Zara this afternoon over at the Catch."

"You mean Earl-Anthony."

"Should I come back and get you?"

"I don't think so, hon. Just say I said . . . hello."

"I will," he said softly. "I will."

And so as Brando drove down the hill, he thought what might have been for Selma Fant. Back in the day she had been one of the top realtors and interior designers in the city. She had even brokered his house. Back in the day she had been sober and happy. But years of guilt can be a debilitating thing, a cancer, curable only by self-forgiveness.

Selma Fant had become a guilt-ridden drunk, and once again she would miss the chance to hear Miss Zara sing.

Chapter Two

I don't get it," Vanessa Ellerbee said, seemingly to the wall her husband, William, had slouched against. "Make me understand, William." But he still said nothing. His freshened appearance and the whiff of Escape spoke volumes. He had sprayed on Cool Water when he left the house ten hours earlier. And he smelled of Irish Spring, not Ivory, which he showered with before he left home. Finally and slowly he lifted his face and stared at her with a look that said, "What's to understand that you don't understand already?"

Knowing full well what he meant by the stare, Vanessa threw up her hands and shook her head full of church-ready curls. With weary disgust she sucked on her teeth and shifted her weight from one side to the other and sighed as she always sighed whenever he returned home wearing new soap and cologne.

"I'm not letting you go," she vowed like the fool she knew she had become.

"I have no intention of leaving. The congregation wouldn't understand."

"Go get dressed," she then said.

"Are we going to Lucy Florence afterwards?"

"Do the twins serve pie?"

And while William dressed in the suit Vanessa had laid out for him, she stormed out of the bedroom, down the staircase, and stared at herself in the foyer mirror. She was still beautiful and alluring, still intelligent and articulate. But was she still the unconventional freethinker who had not thought her marriage would be hindered by her husband's bisexuality? He had been up-front with her right from the beginning. And she had gone along with it, encouraged it even. William was a great lover who was even better after being with a man. She loved watching her husband getting fucked and then getting hers afterward.

But things had changed. She missed DuPré Dixon almost as much as her husband did.

DuPré Dixon, who William had met in a chat room, was one of those slim, torpedo-dick dream pops who smiled like a happy drunk when he fucked, and fucked like good samba when he drank. Her husband loved being fucked by a drunken DuPré, and though she enjoyed the show as much as the sex she got later, she began to suspect that her husband liked getting fucked by DuPré a little too much.

But those suspicions she soon set aside. For no matter how good it was for her husband, it was simply the sex that made DuPré deliver. DuPré was not about to fall in love with William. He was in it just for the intrigue, for the hell of it, for the freaky thrill, for the pussy, no matter who was wearing it. DuPré loved his women like he loved his men like he loved his drink. And on more than a few occasions, Vanessa got in on the action as well. For DuPré, having this beautiful couple, these beautiful bookends, was almost as good as a fantasy threesome with Halle and Shamar.

And DuPré was highly discreet and not curious. He came over only for sex, not conversation, not friendship, not romance. He never asked about hometowns, hobbies, or occupations, nor was any information volunteered.

But DuPré was gone now, having driven home drunk once too often, having lost his head rear-ending an eighteen-wheeler while his convertible top was down, making a mess on the 405 freeway. Gone. The one man that could keep Vanessa's man home, that would fuck him then hand him back over. Gone. And she was scared.

After DuPré, William went out often and got with God-knows-who. As wild as their times with DuPré were, their sexual encounters never occurred outside the privacy of their Ladera Heights home. They had to be very careful, for they had reputation and standing to protect. Everyone knew Reverend and Mrs. Ellerbee as the perfect couple, a shining example of love and devotion for the community and the congregation that William shepherded.

All throughout church service Vanessa listened from the front pew as her husband preached with a fervor so intense that she could not help but think of the man he had been with last night; how good it must have been to fire him up like this, to have him prancing in the pulpit as he'd never pranced before, laughing and humming and writhing like a holy roller.

And while the church rocked to the thunder in his voice, she found herself rocking, too, shivering with fear and jealousy, moaning with an anguish those around her thought was spirit caught up by the good preacher's wife.

She broke into tears out of nowhere. She threw up her hands and wailed loudly. The tongues that she spoke in cursed her husband the reverend for who he was and how he was, and cursed herself for letting it be.

She jumped up from the pew and stomp-danced in a circle, balled up her fists, and beat on her breasts. The nurse's attendants came to her rescue and wrestled her down.

And then Reverend William James Ellerbee called on the choir to make joyful noise.

Chapter Three

When Charlene Alexander opened the front door, her husband, Ramon, was still seated naked on the couch, his hand absently probing his balls and dick, eyes glued to the TV.

"Where the hell you been all this time?" he said without looking up.

"I told you I'm in charge of the nursery now, so I stay for both services."

"I don't remember you telling me that."

"Told you last week."

"You ain't told me jack!" he yelled at her angrily, looking up and glaring at her long enough to warn her.

"Look, Ramon, I just left church and I'm in no mood to come down off my high."

"Yeah, you could use a little Jesus. Probably fuckin' the minister. All you church bitches be fuckin' the minister."

"Why aren't you dressed?" It was bad enough Ramon never wanted to go to church with her, but blasphemy got to her, not as much as it used to, for she long ago recognized that her husband was going straight to hell. "I thought you were going to be dressed when I got back."

"Dressed for what?"

"We're not going to Roscoe's?"

"I ain't feelin' no damn chicken and waffles."

"I wish you would've told me when we first talked about it this morning. I could've gone there by myself straight from church."

"Yeah, to hook up with your preacher man?"

"Gimme some money. I left my change in the collection plate."

"Use your Visa. I need my cash."

"For what? Where are you going?"

"I'm hangin' with Tyler. We're going to the tracks."

"The way you two hang you'd think you were doing each other."

"Look, bitch, don't be talkin' that faggot shit to me."

"I'm not going to be too many more of your bitches, Ramon."

"I hate them mothafuckin' perverts."

She walked over to the couch and sighed.

"Ramon, what is this?"

"What?"

"You got cum stains on the damn couch."

"Ain't this shit got Scotchgard on it?"

"Why do you have to sit here naked, masturbating all over the damn place?"

"'Cause I'm a man with a fuckin' dick, goddamnit!"

"You're an idiot."

"What did you say?"

"You're a—"

But before she could get it out, he jumped up and knocked

her to the floor. He stood over her, huffing; the slit of his dick was staring her down.

"I ain't no fuckin' faggot and I ain't no fuckin' idiot. You understand me, bitch?"

Her face was too swollen for her to speak. She trembled with anger and fear. She got up off the floor and pushed him aside, then marched into the kitchen.

He sat back down on the sofa and grumbled profanities. Moments later, she was back in the room, a butcher's knife in her hand. She came up behind him, grabbed a scrub of his hair, snatched back his head, and put the blade firmly to his neck. He froze . . . then he smiled.

"One day, you gone actually have the guts to use that thing."

But today was not that day. She lowered the knife and let it drop from her trembling hand. She then ran into the bedroom, threw herself on the bed, and cried for all she had lost.

He entered the bedroom and lay down beside her. She tensed when he touched her.

"Why you make me do shit to you?" he whispered. And just for a moment he was that gentle bear of a man she had fallen in love with, had married, had seen go off to war, and who had returned a cold, heartless monster she now needed to leave, but couldn't.

Chapter Four

At First AME Church, Brando hugged his parents after service and told them he'd see them later at dinner. He then circulated through the crowd of parishioners he had known all his life.

Mr. and Mrs. Heywood found Everene Dempsey near the water cooler right outside the sanctuary door and chatted cheerfully with her and her newly divorced daughter, Dee, who had recently moved back to L.A. from New York. As usual, the Heywoods were selling their prized son on the gentle hush, pointing him out to the new divorcée with grinning pride. Although years ago they accepted the fact that their only child was gay, they still hoped that one day he might swerve against his nature and give them the grandchild they so desperately craved.

Dee sympathized with the Heywoods. Yes, their son was a handsome and seemingly upright gentleman that any woman would want to have, but as Dee observed him chatting with friends on the other side of the sanctuary, her gaydar kicked in.

Not that Brando gave any physical indication, but Dee,

with many gay friends in the entertainment industry on both coasts, and an openly gay brother with whom she was very close, had a sixth sense. She was rarely ever wrong.

She watched fondly as Brando and his friends talked. She perceived that they were all gay, albeit unreadable to the average observer, except for the older gentleman who appeared to be dominating the conversation with elegantly effeminate hand gestures, an occasional finger snap, and a breezy flamboyancy that caused an usher gathering songbooks nearby to shake his head before catching himself in a temporary state of political incorrectness.

"Now, the invitations to my winter supper are going in the mail tomorrow and I expect each and every one of you to RSVP instead of just showing up, like some of you are known to do," Senior Father Lacey Cannon said, eyeing Cedric Warfield beneath an arched eyebrow. All his gay friends called him Senior Father because of his history. Having been one of the rioting patrons who stood up to the police at New York's Stonewall bar back in 1969, an act that ignited the gay revolution, Lacey Cannon was a bona fide pioneer of the movement.

"Why are you eyeballing *me*, Senior Father?" protested Cedric.

"Because I know how you are, chile. And it's for you and *a* guest," he reminded them all. "*A* as in *one*. And I don't want to see any of you draggin' no triflin' ghetto trade up to my house either. That goes for everybody except for Brando."

"Huh?"

"You can bring whoever you want, baby doll. Po' thing ain't had a date in a month of Sundays."

"I'm sure I'll be coming alone," Brando said.

"You are such a waste, chile. A gorgeous piece of work like you? You don't even need to be alone."

"I'm fine, Senior Father. Thank you for your concern."

"And what's up with you, Shane?" Senior Father scolded lightly. "Why you got your lip all stuck out?"

"Omar," Cedric volunteered. "He hasn't seen him all week."

"Well, where is he keeping himself?"

"Ask his man," Shane answered with a snarl. His Puerto Rican accent added a sting as he stared hard at Brando with accusatory eyes. "He know better than me."

Shane Santos did not dislike Brando—on the contrary—but he was jealous of him and the time Brando and Omar spent together. And anyone who knew the two knew that Omar had feelings for Brando that went beyond friendship, feelings Omar tried hard to mask.

"Oh no." Brando stared back innocently. "I'm not in that."

Cedric chuckled. "You're not into anything these days."

"Isn't Clymenthia Teager signing at Eso Won tonight?" Senior Father asked. His well-known messiness was beginning to surface.

"Yes," Brando answered tentatively, knowing where this was going.

"Clock his behind there," Senior Father said to Shane with a sweeping hand.

"What time?" Shane was dead serious.

"Seven," Senior Father offered with delight.

"This oughta be good," Cedric mused.

"See, y'all are not right," Brando said, walking away and giving them the hand.

"No, yo' best friend the one ain't right," Shane called out to his back.

From across the room, Dee noted the gentle drama with amusement.

Chapter Five

At the Lucy Florence Coffeehouse on Degnan Boulevard, in that quaint part of the city known as the African Village, Omar and Brando met at exactly a quarter past one. They found their usual table on the upper level overlooking the stage. They ordered coffee and sweet potato pie from one of the identical-twin owners.

The night that Omar's grandmother died, the night he spent crying in Brando's arms, was the night Omar fell in love with Brando. And after more than twenty years, it was a love that remained undeclared and unrequited, though often hinted at.

In time Omar had somehow learned to accept an oblivious Brando as a platonic friend who, perhaps, would never know that once upon a time he had inadvertently broken Omar's heart with an offer of friendship when romance was the secret caller on the line.

Omar and Brando had different occupations in the same industry. Brando was an entertainment lawyer who represented a disparate group of clients, from rappers to literary writers. He had just signed Clymenthia Teager to a high-six-figure three-book deal on the strength of her current best-selling award winner. Omar Stevens was a showbiz writer and journalist.

In the two years since his and Collier's breakup, Brando found himself running the streets and hitting the clubs with Omar more often than he'd liked (although he did get off on shaking his booty on the dance floor of Boy Trade, the first-Friday-night-of-the-month disco throwdown for L.A.'s black and Latino gay crowd. At Boy Trade Brando and Omar were usually the oldest folks in the house).

"His name is Thomas," Omar reported on his latest side piece while the other twin served their coffee and pie. "He's a track runner at San Diego State. Comes up to L.A. every other weekend. Calls me at the last minute. Tells me to be at such-and-such motel, and I'm there, 'cause the boy is no joke. I cry it's so good. Ass sweeter than wine. Dick melts in your mouth. Just thinking about him gets me hot enough to wanna fuck you."

"I don't know why you're always trying to shock me." Brando laughed.

"Rattle yo' borin' ass up."

"Uh-huh."

"So anyway, he's back in town now, for good. He's living with his mother in Compton. So what am I supposed to do? How am I going to juggle him and Shane?"

"I don't know, but you need to do something," Brando said. "I'm the one getting shade from Shane."

"He's jealous."

"Jealous?" Brando asked innocently, as if he didn't know.

"Yeah. Of you."

"Why?"

Omar chose to ignore the question.

"He called this morning. Left a message on my voicemail. Said he missed the sound of my voice. Damn. Now see, that's a good boyfriend. Not lover. We're not there yet. We just crossed over from fuck buddies."

"Does *he* know this?"

"He knows, but you know how he is. He's one of them anal-possessive New York Negro-Ricans, with his phine-ass self."

"I guess."

"We have an arrangement."

"Okay."

"While we're seeing each other, we can see others, too. We just don't need to talk about it."

"And he agreed to that?"

"Yep."

"Damn, bro, what you got down there?"

"Oh, so now you don't remember, huh?"

Brando remembered, all right. And he smiled at the long-ago memory. It had happened right before Brando headed east to college. They had been celebrating at Omar's place, the house his Grammy had left him. And they had gotten pissy drunk. Prince blasted through the speakers of the stereo and the two eighteen-year-olds, toned by youth and high school athletics, laughingly danced around the living room in their tight white briefs, playing matching air guitars like a pair of chocolate Tom Cruises in *Risky Business*.

The drunken performance accelerated into a fierce dance-off, which soon became a spastic wrestling match during which white briefs were clumsily shredded and ripped off and two drunken young he-men found themselves tumbling nude and sweaty, grabbing buff biceps and stiff nipples, being beat in the face with hard dicks and moist assholes, humping each other like yard dogs in heat, biting and sucking on everything they had, fucking each other with their dicks and their tongues, exhausting each other with a pleasure so nasty that they fell dead to sleep in the damp funk of their teenage pungency.

They woke up the next morning with big hangovers and deliberate amnesia.

Over the years they would never speak of the event directly, only in innuendos, giggly asides, and rhetorical questions. They were both afraid to explore too deeply the wild sexual intimacy they enjoyed that one and only night, an intimacy Brando thought could breach the sacredness of their friendship, an intimacy Omar longed for but was afraid to ask for. For the time being, Omar was content with Thomas the track runner, Shane the boyfriend, and all the other stand-ins for the man he had been in love with for more than two decades.

"With the track runner back in town for good," he continued his tale, "when he called this morning I went; skipped right on over there and did the brotha's cookies. He had just dropped his mother off at the mall and wouldn't have to pick her up for a couple of hours, and he was hot; wanted me over there ten minutes ago. So like a trained show dog I went and did tricks and got me my biscuit treat—"

"While Shane sits up in church giving me the evil eye."

"Evil is where evil lives."

"Watch it, man. Respect."

"Sorry, Bran, but you church children really get me." Omar suddenly thought about his mother and stifled a cringe.

"Omar, you're a godless heathen," Brando half joked.

"I just choose to fear my God outside the temples of commerce and haughtiness."

"And how old is he again?"

"Who?"

"*Who we talkin 'bout, Willis?*"

"The track runner?"

"Yes. Thomas the track runner."

"Twenty-three; something like that."

"That's pretty damn young, Omar."

"Pretty damn young for who?"

"Pretty damn young for your forty-one-year-old ass."

"Look, when I go, I want that scene right out of *The Color Purple* when Whoopi asks that young girl, 'How'd he go?' and the young girl looks up from her hanky and says, 'On top of me.' That's how I'm going, on top of something young, dumb, and full of cum."

"You're crazy."

"And you're a prude, my brotha. How you been able to go without sex for two years is beyond me."

"Everybody wants sex. Nobody wants love."

"Yeah right. That's some shit fat ugly dudes with bad teeth be talkin' over in the corner."

"*Be* talkin'?"

"You must be beatin' that meat like crazy," Omar slipped.

"You don't have any self-control, Omar. Face it. You're a sex addict."

"Why you always gotta be sayin' that to me?"

"Because it's true. You need to really check yourself."

"Nah, you need to really check *yo'self*."

"Hey, I've been celibate for two years."

"That's what you need to be checkin'. That ain't healthy, cuz, building all that shit up inside. And no intimate contact? People ain't built that way. People are built to touch. People are built to fuck."

"Twenty-four-seven?"

"Wish the fuck I could."

"See? Now that's what I'm talking about."

"You know something, Brando?"

"What?"

"You one prudish mothafucka."

"Okay, okay, okay. I'll tell you what."

"What?"

"Go a month without sex and I'll let you make love to me."

"What?" Omar stopped midgulp, not believing what he had just heard.

"It's been a long time. We've been friends a long time. I think we have a pretty good lock on some of our . . . wants, discussed and otherwise. So yes. You go a month without sex and I'll let you make love to me. That's what you want, isn't it?"

"Man, git the fuck outta here with that!"

"Isn't it?"

"Wassup with you, Brando? Talkin' this shit. This ain't you, man."

"Of course it's me. Who else could it be?"

And that's when Omar realized he was dreaming; daydreaming, right in his best friend's face; fantasizing and wanting so badly he could hear "yes" as clear as wind chimes in a silent breeze. Who was he fooling? Certainly not himself. He still hadn't gotten over Brando.

Brando laughed and shook his head at his hopeless and lustful friend, although he was not fully aware, or did not let himself be fully aware, of what his friend was lusting for. After all, he, Brando, had feelings of his own, suppressed feelings that he didn't always understand.

And that's when he could feel it again. The eyes, so fixed that they burned. No. Warmed. Eyes that had found him again this week, just like last Sunday and the Sunday before. Eyes he had caught in the midst of a stare quickly averted; eyes from across the other side of the room.

She was almost as beautiful as the man that she sat with. It was a beauty that was storybook-like, enhanced by the glow of sunshine that streamed in from behind her through the side picture window, bathing her in sepia and gold, dancing lightly, iridescently, amidst her church curls.

And with her eyes she flirted like the delicate lady it was clear that she was—her high-collared blouse, her ever-so-slight smile, her legs that gently crossed, then uncrossed, underneath her soft linen skirt. She turned slightly away as she conspired with her handsome companion with a sad laughing whisper that made him blush with a deep dimpled smile and a nod that was not meant for her.

And although Brando respectfully acknowledged the lady's glance and the gentleman's suggestive nod, he could not help but chuckle inside, wondering what it was about himself that made men smile only from a distance.

A block away, on that tiny grassy island known as Leimert Park, the half dozen drummers began their performance, their weekly ritual that soothed and reminded that this was the African Village.

Chapter Six

At Crenshaw and Jefferson boulevards Brando slowed down and stopped to let a sea of elegant church folk cross. Service had just let out at West Angeles Cathedral. A little girl with glistening burnt-red dreds and delicately dressed in the Westernized garb of a Ghanaian princess smiled at him, as did her stunning mother, who held her hand and led the way to Stevie's on the Strip across the street.

Miss Zara singing at the Catch this afternoon was a treat Brando did not want to miss. Omar was supposed to join him, but had booked a last-minute booty call.

Brando thought about what Omar had said—that he was a prude. He then dismissed the thought. Then Collier came to mind, something he said during one of their rare verbal sparrings shortly after the breakup.

"Why did we spend ten years together?"

"I thought because we loved each other."

"I loved *you*, Brando. You *liked* me. Liked. Not loved."

"I saw it differently."

"Did you? You saw it the way you see everything. I mean, why did you switch to entertainment law when your aptitude for criminal law is at genius level? You're like a brilliant brain surgeon who can't stand the sight of blood."

"That's not true, Collier, and I resent you saying that," Brando snapped.

"It *is* true. You can't stand the sight of life, Bran. You're your parents' perfect son, Omar's perfect friend, some diva fag hag of the future's perfect gay running buddy."

"Why are you saying this to me?"

"Because I loved you. I love you, Brando. God, how I missed what we could've had. Did you know that in ten years you never once said that you loved me?"

And that was the most painful blow of all. He knew that Collier had to be wrong. He wracked his brain to recall one time, one moment—on a birthday, at their commitment ceremony, during sex, at the dinner table, in a darkened movie theater—and feared that Collier might be right.

He continued the drive down Crenshaw Boulevard, thinking, if only he had it to do all over again.

He turned right onto Pico and then after two blocks made a left into the driveway of Jewel's Catch One. Jonestha, the butch-elegant security guard, threw him a tough smile and a high five when he pulled into the packed parking lot. Out on the patio, smokers, banished like lepers, fed their addiction quickly, dowsing half-smoked cigarettes as the band striking up inside the club alerted them to their mission on this very special afternoon.

Miss Zara's fans were like picnic ants. They came in well-formed droves when they got even a whiff of a rumor that she would be singing.

Brando walked through the door with his usual warm smile

that hid thoughts of Collier and his own inadequacies. His public, unassuming demeanor made brothas hot full of dreams and lesbian couples friendly in hopes of scoring quality DNA.

Lucian, the Belizean straight boy who loved hanging out with the gay boys because where gay boys gathered, phine-ass straight girls hung, was tending bar along with Eddie and Carlos, a couple since high school.

The stool, center bar, Brando's stool, was somehow, and as usual, unoccupied in this packed room, so he slid coolly onto it with the ease and the familiarity that warmed him to all those who sat around him and seemed to know and adore him. Someone sent him a drink.

Miss Zara, the grand, vintage transgender diva, then took the stage and the house went up and shook with screams, applause, and whistles. It was then brought to a sudden hush when she threw back her flawless Korean 100 percent human hair weave and, in a voice as rich and as natural as her flawless beauty, she gave it her all and sang "I Who Have Nothing."

To those from the old school, Miss Zara was Sir Lady Java with voice. No lip-synch here. And what a voice. The biological maleness beneath the feminine contributed a bass that made what would have been pure female contralto bourbon gold. And not one shaky note. She had vibrato, a hypnotic vocal shimmy that played with you like a tango, that made you touch yourself and pinch your nipples, then tossed you away when you tried to lick it. She was more than a mere drag queen supreme. She was pure Kabuki soul.

Brando sat there, all melancholy smiles, watching her, remembering her, remembering back to almost twenty years ago.

The first time he fell in love with her. The first time he fell in love with him. And the first time he got his heart broken.

He was home during Christmas break from Howard University. The Fants, like Brando's parents, were a part of the powerful liberal black, Jewish, and gay political coalition that dominated Los Angeles politics. In a city where only 11 percent of the population was African American, African American Tom Bradley, first elected mayor in 1972, served five unprecedented terms.

The Heywoods, eager to nourish their bright but shy son with hearty doses of community activism and liberal politics, brought Brando to one of the Fants' well-orchestrated Sunday-afternoon mixers, a grassroots fund-raiser for Mayor Bradley, poolside at the Fants' family home.

And there he was—Brando was transfixed—the beautiful church boy with the voice of an angel and a devil's self-confidence, whose show-stopping performance urged many of the visitors to write checks larger than what they had planned. And the beautiful church boy was all smiles and pizzazz as he basked in the adoration of the crowd. Even Mayor Bradley, tall, cool, and straitlaced, had to put a hand on a hip and shake his head from side to side and let out a "Well-awright-now!" when the beautiful church boy sang in a voice that was almost profane in its power and brilliance.

Brando, far back in the crowd, was dumbstruck, smitten by the voice and the demeanor and the face and the light of the Fants' only child.

And even as the beautiful church boy took it all in with a graciousness greater than his age, he did indeed catch Brando out of the corner of his eye, and they saw each other.

At eighteen, Earl-Anthony Fant was many things. His mastery of the keyboard matched the beauty of his voice, and at Gentle Spirit Holy Mother Church he was the undisputed star of the choir. People came from miles around to hear him perform. Even Jehovah's Witnesses, forbidden by doctrine to enter other houses of worship, were found peeking through the doors of Gentle Spirit Holy Mother Church to get an earful of the gift.

That Earl-Anthony Fant was so beautiful, so pretty, so pretty boy perfect, and both sexy and sanctified was just a small part of what drew Brando to him. The spirit of the boy had so taken him that he had to sit down, catch his breath, and calm his racing heart. For a moment he had lost all sense of place and time. He was not aware that the words he heard in his head did not come from him. Someone else was speaking his thoughts.

"You are the most beautiful man I have ever seen in my life."

That's what he heard. And that's what he felt. And while Brando looked up and saw the beautiful church boy sitting across from him, smiling that beautiful church boy smile, riding on the echoes of his beautiful church boy words, words would not come to Brando. Only dumbness. Numbness. And the beautiful church boy understood.

"You really are the most beautiful man I have ever seen in my life," Earl-Anthony said once again, not caring what anyone in earshot could hear.

They became friends, Brando and Earl-Anthony Fant. But Brando was in love. Then again, everyone was in love with Earl-Anthony. Schoolgirls ripped the top of their blouses like Jewish widows whenever he passed. College quarterbacks begged for a sweet taste in the back of the locker room and privately dedicated touchdowns to him. He was Tut and Cleopatra before he was old enough to realize he could be both. He was the one that down-low brothas, too man to take dick, took dick from.

And so Earl-Anthony Fant understood why Brando would take his "You are the most beautiful man I have ever seen" as a declaration of love as opposed to the routine flirtation of an incandescent male diva it was meant to be.

For the two weeks that Brando was home, they became Spartan fuck buddies, Earl-Anthony the teacher, Brando the shy and smitten charge. For Brando the pleasure of the lovemaking was overwhelming. It was different from anything he had ever experienced before. It was different from those middle school sleepovers at Jake Harlan's where they compared dick size and he pretended to sleep while Jake sucked him off underneath the covers. It was different from the high school locker room circle jerks where he and a handful of questioning jocks pretended to get their rocks off by aiming for the Coke bottle in the center of their circle while fantasizing about the big-breasted cheerleaders few of them wanted. It was even different from that drunken encounter with Omar, when he stifled the first real feelings of love.

With Earl-Anthony, it was different. Brando's feelings for Earl-Anthony became nakedly honest and obvious. He loved Earl-Anthony. He was obsessed with Earl-Anthony and understood why all who knew the beautiful church boy worshiped at his feet, on their backs, on their stomachs, on their knees.

When he was with Earl-Anthony, he did not want to let him

go, so deeply had he fallen under the church boy's spell. And when circumstances—singing engagements, choir rehearsals, servicing others—forced them to be apart, Brando spent his every waking hour with thoughts of him, profusely wacking off to visions of him. Sleep was filled with dreams of him.

Brando searched the city high and low, and finally, at the Pleasure Dome, a sex shop on Santa Monica Boulevard in West Hollywood, found a meager surrogate when his need was inconvenient. The nine-inch dildo was the closest match he could find. It resembled Earl-Anthony's beautiful nine-inch penis: perfectly cut, flared like a slitted, almond-colored mushroom, with thick veins like those that pulsated Earl-Anthony's beautiful dick into action readiness.

"I love you, Earl-Anthony," Brando said on their final night together, the night before he was to return to Washington, D.C.

"No, you don't. You love what you allow yourself to be when we're together. When you go back to school, you'll look back on this as a wonderful chapter in your life that will help you explore your life more fully."

"I want to just be with you."

"You haven't experienced enough, Brando, to know that this is it, that I'm it. I know I certainly haven't. I'm in the process of exploring the world. I'm in the process of exploring myself. When I come to know me, more fully, then I'll come to love me, more fully. And only then will I be able to love someone else the way they truly need to be loved. In the meantime, enjoy the journey. You'll know your destination when you get there."

Brando cried during most of the six-hour flight back to D.C., having lost his first great love before even possessing it.

He cried himself to sleep the first three nights back at the dorm. His roommate, Ted, panicked the first night, shook him the second, and on the third snatched him out of bed, threw him against the wall, and called him a wailing-ass bitch.

He got up that night and looked at himself in the mirror and realized that that's exactly what he had become, a wailing-ass bitch. He wiped away the snot and put Visine in his eyes and apologized to Ted.

These feelings for Earl-Anthony had taken him over, and slowly he determined that he had to survive this, and take this as a lesson—a lesson he learned almost too well.

Brando now regarded love cautiously, with a near-icy deference. The wound healed over and the scab hardened. To avoid the pain of love, he did not allow himself to love deeply enough for love to breathe, rise up, and take aim ever again. Maybe Collier was right.

The things you remember. The things you regret. The things you forgive yourself for. The things you do not.

And now, as he listened to Miss Zara sing, remembering her as Earl-Anthony, Brando's smile was filled with a sadness that no one else in the club would have noticed or understood. But he understood. It was about more than the sweet vision of Earl-Anthony, buried in Miss Zara's performance, that conjured so wonderful and painful a memory of love experienced, flashed, star-crossed, then fizzled like a Fourth of July sparkler. It was about what he had become.

When he began to cry, no one really noticed. After all, that's what Miss Zara did to people—made them cry and made them love her all over again.

40

Chapter Seven

On one level, Omar Stevens considered himself too old to hang out with all the young guys half his age in Griffith Park on Sunday afternoons, despite the fact that Griffith Park on Sunday afternoons was where the chickens of his carnal desire cooped. He did truly love the young, and they truly seemed to love him. He was as good a lay as any of them, and he was good with the gifts. He provided drinks, pricey dinners at chic Beverly Hills eateries, electronic gear, pocket change, weekend trips to Vegas, San Francisco, and Mazatlán, and a Caribbean cruise for the especially gifted. And they always thanked him in the very best ways.

So Griffith Park was where Omar hung on Sunday afternoons. And Griffith Park was where Omar met twenty-year-old Andrew several Sundays back.

Andrew was simply beautiful, a finely chiseled, thick-lipped, high-cheekboned thug prince. He always had his scowl fixed, his head cocked, and his pants down. Outside of his dress and demeanor, he looked like most of the boys Omar dated, just another variation of Brando.

Andrew lived across town in Silver Lake, right above Sunset

Boulevard on Micheltorena. Omar figured he could knock that out real quick and still have plenty of time to get back over to La Brea and Rodeo Road in Baldwin Hills for his interview with Clymenthia Teager prior to her reading and signing.

Whenever Omar and Andrew got together they got right down to business. Omar would ring the doorbell. Moments later Andrew would snatch the door open and pose threateningly—the ghetto stance, the thick tongue licking glistening, half-parted lips, the low-hanging jeans held up only by a high-hoisted ass and a huge wad of dick. He would stand there long enough for Omar to take in the vision.

Then they would attack each other with hungry-man kisses and door slamming caused by the impact of twirl-grinding and groping and grunting and wrestling and tumbling toward the bedroom. They would leave a shambled trail of Reeboks and Florsheims and 501s and Armanis and wife beaters. Burberry briefs and cheap polyester boxers would be stomped off to the ground. They would suck on nipples like newborns, take to dick like the bottle. Hot breath would heat up both pairs of balls, and Omar's tongue, with decades of experience, would play gently around the soft, trim hairs that circled the sweet smiling young pucker.

Young stallion legs would hoist up and spread young ass for old dick that now begged for a ride with a quiver, and young ass would oblige with the joy of the pain that only good, deep penetration brings.

Two dicks, hard, one bobbing and dripping with the joy of getting it good, the other a chocolate torpedo, almost too big for the ultrasheer Maxx condom, a beautiful blue-black hot dreamsicle, giving it with the greatest of ease.

Fingers scratched walls; eyes shimmied underneath fluttering eyelids. The young boy's earlier scowl became an eye-bulging grimace of unbearable pleasure from getting slam-dunked with a swift steady rhythm. He oohed and he aahed and he moaned and he grunted with uncool abandon and glee.

"Oh shit, mothafucka!" he screeched, slamming himself on the dick that impaled him. "Yeah, daddy. That's right! Git you that ass! Git you that ass! *Get you that good boy-pussy ass, mothafucka! Ooh! Ah! Grrrr!*"

Andrew had to confess that Omar was pretty hot for a bourgie Ladera Heights o.g. Omar knew how to wear the young ones out beyond satisfaction, leaving them begging for more. And Andrew wanted more. He knew that the first time Omar fucked him. But deep down inside he knew that all he could be to Omar was just another young piece, looking for dick, dollars, and daddy, and that was cool. It would have to be.

"Damn, niggah, that was tight."

"Omar. The name's Omar."

"Whatever," Andrew said with a half chuckle. He then took a soothing drag off his blunt. "You wanna hit offa this?"

"Nah, man, I'm working today. I'm covering a book signing."

"A what?"

Omar leaned over and answered him with a kiss. Oh how he liked them young, dumb, and full of cum.

Chapter Eight

Shane knew that he had no real reason to be pissed off at Omar. Omar had not really lied to him, and never made any promises to him except that they would have some fun times together.

Well, maybe that was the lie. Fun times together? Fun times with Omar had diminished ever since they decided to be boyfriends, ever since Shane insisted that their relationship be more than what it was and more than what Omar was at first willing to offer.

But Omar was as afraid of losing Shane as Shane was of being lost. Shane knew that much. He was Omar's emotional security blanket, the one guy that would always love him, not just for the sex, not just for the trinkets, the trips, the wild times, but for those quiet times when Omar didn't have to be "on." Shane loved him enough to occasionally read his ass the riot act, tell him no, tell him things for his own good, things he didn't want to hear but needed to hear.

Oh yeah, Shane realized that Omar was a dog. But at least he was an honest dog. An immature, sometimes selfish, often impetuous, mostly lovable dog. Omar had been totally up-front about the other guys in his life, his need for an open relationship, his need to have his cake and eat it too, and Shane thought he could handle it. They had even negotiated terms: absolutely no barebacking. Just as they had always used condoms, Omar would always use condoms with anybody else. And Omar would never bring anyone home to his place. Shane would be the only one to share Omar's bed, and vice versa. That was an easy deal for Shane. For him, there *was* nobody else. And yet, it was not so easy.

He knew that he had, more or less, pressured Omar into this "boyfriend" thing. That was the only way Shane was going to stick around, or at least that was his threat. Even though he knew that he was Omar's special guy, he wanted to be Omar's only guy, and often felt cheated and compromised.

He had no one else to blame but himself, taking this shit, loving this motherfucker so.

He wasn't even sure what he wanted from Omar anymore. To love him back equally? All he knew was that he wanted more than what he was getting.

If only he was Brando.

Shane knew that as long as Brando was in the picture, he could be no more than a second thought.

But then again, anybody who wanted to be with Omar, and there were many who did, could only be a second thought. Guys like Andrew the Silver Lake thug prince and Thomas the Compton track runner were pesky distractions.

But Brando . . .

Everybody knew but nobody said anything. It was an open secret. Brando and Omar were lovers, and didn't even know it.

"So since you're not answering your cell I guess you're

busy, huh?" Shane said into his phone, as if the voicemail would answer him back. "Am I gonna see you today? Call me."

For just a second, Shane thought about driving over to Omar's place. For just a second—and then he thought a second longer and changed his mind. That was just a bit too desperate. It was times like this when he could really use a drink. But he knew better. His life depended on it.

And it was his life that suddenly flashed before him as he slammed on the brakes and swerved his car, barely missing the gray Nissan Altima running the light. Angrily he pounded the horn and cursed the vanishing vehicle in Spanglish.

But Ramon Alexander, the Nissan's driver, could give less than a damn. Ramon laughed when he looked over and saw Tyler, ashen-faced, in the passenger seat. "Man, what you sweatin' for?"

"You coulda fuckin' killed us!" Tyler screamed.

"Then let's go celebrate with some pussy. My treat."

"What?"

"Pussy, man, pussy! Hit the daily double, get yo'self some pussy and die!"

Hollywood Park had been good to Ramon. The horses were running his way, which was more than what could be said for Tyler, who had lost his whole paycheck and was not in the mood.

"You fuckin' stupid, man, you know that?"

"Hey, don't be callin' me stupid, man. I don't wanna have to—"

"What? Beat me down like you do your wife?" Tyler shot back. "I don't think so."

"What goes on between me and my bitch ain'tcha fuckin' business, you know?"

"Got that right," Tyler muttered, wondering why he even bothered to hang out with this moron. But he knew why. He owed him. He owed him his very life. He never would have made it out of Kuwait if it hadn't been for Ramon.

Ramon softened up a bit. "Hey, man, come on. We each other's boy, right? We got each other's back, don't we?"

"Say what?"

"Don't we?"

"I guess," said Tyler, resigned, thinking back to the last time he sweated like this.

"You fuckin' my husband?" Charlene Alexander had asked him point-blank, surprising and not surprising him at what sometimes comes out of the mouths of the most holy.

"Say what?" he had answered her, just as he answered Ramon, but more truthfully. After all, wishing is not doing.

Ramon pulled out his cell phone and made two calls. After the second call he snapped his phone shut victoriously.

"It's on," he declared, extending his hand for the brotha man slap Tyler robotically gave him. "They gone meet us at the motel in ten minutes."

It was funny and sad, Tyler thought to himself. Women never turned Ramon Alexander down. No woman ever dared.

Gelisa and Tammy were waiting, ready, and naked when Ramon and Tyler arrived.

"I'mo take Tammy," Ramon told Tyler as he unbuttoned

his shirt with a nasty smile and eyes keen to Tammy's thick auburn bush. Tammy smiled nasty back as she slowly strolled toward him. His shirt fell to the ground, and while she unbuttoned his belt buckle his fingers slipped deep into the warm dampness between her legs. He kicked off his pants, then she pulled him on top of her on one of the beds. He bit at her titties and rammed himself roughly inside her. She buckled and moaned with the pain he had every intention of giving.

Tyler stood there transfixed. The sight of Ramon's massive hairy-slit ass flexing and pounding that auburn bush had taken his breath away and hardened his dick toward near busting.

"You like to watch, huh?"

He jumped, startled by Gelisa's hot breath in his ear.

"Huh?"

"You like to watch," she whispered again, her hard-nippled breasts stabbing his back, her naked body engulfing him tightly from behind, her hands around his waist, discovering his rock-hard dick nearly tearing its way out of his pants. She found his zipper and gave his dick its freedom while he tried hard not to look at his homeboy's behind.

He turned and faced Gelisa. She looked him in the eye, seductively, challengingly, then whispered it again: "You like to watch. You do, don't you?"

"Fuck that shit," he whispered back, and hoisted her naked body onto the dresser. He spread her legs and let her guide him deep inside her. Pressed against the dresser mirror, she closed her eyes and filled herself with everything he had. And so he started slow and steady. Then the reflection in the mirror caught his eye; that massive hairy-slit ass, flexing and pounding, flexing and pounding. And now he was flexing and pounding Gelisa, fucking her spread-eagled on the dresser like there was no tomorrow, fucking her so good she forgot she was doing it for money, fucking her as if he was fucking that hairy-slit ass in the mirror.

Chapter Nine

The "children" whistled and screamed and begged as she brought her third encore to a rousing gospel finale. They were standing on chairs and chanting her name and tossing flowers and tens and twenties at her feet. They were relentless in not letting her get away. But as she smiled that million-dollar smile and tossed kisses with a Queen Elizabeth wave, she moved gracefully sideways, head perfectly tilted, and grandly backed upstage left until the bright golden light made her silhouette appear as an angel in flames. Her light and her flame grew brighter and brighter until she became too hard to look at and her image exploded magnificently and all became black. When the house lights came up, Miss Zara was gone.

Backstage, Miss Zara's husband, Eli, helped her undress, counted her money, and told her how fabulous she was. Miss Zara gave her gentle giant a gentle kiss, just as he liked it. He had already laid out her receiving gown. As was the ritual, he would allow her time to ponder and soak in the love of her fans—and this night, the love of a friend she had not seen in ages.

Brando.

It was good seeing him in the house, good seeing him again. Seeing him made her think about home, and Mom and Dad . . . and Peter. Peter Caise. And why she left home to begin with. Eli understood, had always understood; and so after massaging her back with a soothing only he knew how to give, he left her to the bittersweet memories she dealt with as best she could. And that's what he loved so much about her— she was the diva indeed, the diva of love and all its wonderful terrible ups and downs, a learned diva who had studied and learned her life lessons well.

Out on the floor, exhausted and spent, the crowd "chile'd" one another and giddily struggled to find words to describe the magnificence of Miss Zara.

Brando could not move from his stool. New tears glazed his eyes while old tears streamed down his cheeks. It was good to see Miss Zara again. She had even sung a song to him, and he was glad that they somehow had remained friends, even if distant, all these years.

"I see she really got to you," the woman said.

"She always does," he answered, smiling toward the empty stage without looking toward the voice, without wiping away the tears, caught up in the sweet aftertaste of magic and memory. "She is truly all that."

"You know her personally?"

"We go way back."

"You know, we see each other all the time—you and I— but we've never spoken."

And it was then that Brando turned toward the voice. It

was her. He could not resist a subtle glance around the room for her companion.

"Right," he finally said with a new smile of cordial recognition. "Lucy Florence Coffeehouse,"

"Exactly. Vanessa Ellerbee."

"Brando. Brando Heywood."

"May I buy you a drink, Brando?"

"Thanks, but I'm driving. Folks have been buying me drinks all afternoon."

"So I noticed."

"Okay."

"We both did," she then said knowingly. "He's over there at the table by the wall. He's not as comfortable in places like this. He's very discreet, and shy."

"Is he, now?"

"Yes, as well as being very . . ."

"Very . . . ," Brando urged casually.

"So listen." Vanessa veered left. "Is that your lover?"

"Who?" Brando questioned with slight surprise, mildly taken aback by the woman's bold straightforwardness.

"The guy you come to the coffeehouse with every Sunday. Your Sunday brunch mate."

"No, just a . . . very good friend."

"He looks like he wants to be more than just your very good friend."

Vanessa knew, when on the prowl, that every nuance must be noted, and even from across the room she could read the language of his companion's heart and body—the stolen glances, the wanting smile, the hidden longing, the look Brando pulled from his desperate brunch mate whenever he got up to go to the men's room, the sadly hopeful sigh he engendered.

"Really?" was all Brando could say to a statement he knew held some truth.

"Look, Im going to be honest with you," she continued. "William—"

"William?"

"My . . . friend." She pointed him out with her eyes. He sat barely discernible in the shadows in the corner. The thick, pitch-black sunglasses did more to attract attention than to hide him, Brando thought to himself. William nodded with a slow cool that Brando returned noncommittally.

"He thinks you're very attractive," Vanessa continued, a sexy smile in her voice. "He's been thinking that since the first time he set eyes on you at Lucy Florence. But he's shy—"

"Too shy—"

"—to introduce himself. Ergo . . ."

"Here *you* are."

"Yes. Here I am."

Brando's keen legal mind began to microassess: this beautiful woman was in this gay club procuring for a man clearly handsome enough to do that for himself. It was a fascinating premise, though Brando's interest was little piqued. In his mind he chose his words carefully. He covered with a smile while he sorted them out and constructed a diplomatic response.

"Yo, man, wassup?" a familiar deep, rich baritone bellowed out from behind him. He turned toward Eli's broad, smiling face and then found himself smothered in the larger man's bear hug.

"Eli."

"You know she waitin' for you."

Brando had not been quite sure how to handle the situation with Vanessa and her friend over by the wall. Though William was handsome, maybe even a nice enough guy, at least from a distance, it was not Brando's style to be approached in this way. He graciously introduced Vanessa to Eli, and then, equally gracious, begged off an introduction to William, at least for the time being.

"Listen, Vanessa, I have to go. I'm sure I'll see you at Lucy Florence soon."

"Next Sunday I'm sure," she said, extending her hand. He kissed it, and then gestured cordially to William against the wall.

And as Brando walked away, in familiar conversation with Eli, Vanessa kept her eyes on him and did not look away until after he had disappeared backstage. Then slowly she turned around and found William. She saw the hunger on his face, even beneath the sunglasses. She reassured him with her stare that promised she would deliver a formidable replacement for the much missed DuPré Dixon. Some for him. And maybe even some for her.

Miss Zara was seated at her vanity, resplendent in her receiving gown, when through her mirror she eyed Brando standing in her dressing room doorway. Eli edged him on and, not coming in himself, pulled the door shut.

Inside the dressing room was a silence, save for the distant beat of good house music. Miss Zara stood slowly, with a mock sultriness. She studied her beautiful mirror image from head to toe and approved. She then turned to her boyish old friend and smiled that smile that was for him alone.

"Chile, when are you going to start shaving?" She grimaced approvingly.

"Whatever happened to a diva saying hello first?" he countered, with a wide, beautiful smile.

"Whatever happened to a Negro coming to a diva's dressing room and telling her how fabulous she was?" she snapped back. "And where's that trollop Omar?"

"To question one: You were absolutely fabulous. To question two: Where else? Where the boys are. I'm supposed to give him a full review, in case you ask."

"*Humph.* Boy can't keep those three inches in his pants to save his life. Come over here and kiss me," she said, stretching her arms out wide, arms that he filled warmly. And they hugged and kissed like old friends and old lovers. Then she leaned back and, in a full and slow gander, undressed him with playful eyes. "Look at you," the deep, sexy voice purred.

"You're the one . . . Your mother said to tell you hello."

"Did she?" Miss Zara responded with a sudden chill. "Is she still doing her Sunday-morning cocktails?"

Chapter Ten

Selma Fant sat in the dark of her private media room, her fine lace panties down around her ankles, draping her Ferragamos like the small gathered train of a bridal gown. With glazed-over, bloodshot, and unblinking eyes, eyes that bulged wildly and drunkenly stillborn under heavy black lashes, she stared at the hot black gay porn on the bright screen before her. She ate popcorn and drank vodka and watched with zombie intent while boys fucked and got fucked and busted nut after nut, one after another, some all together. Big blue-black stallions and hot bubble-butt sissies, and a doggie-style roughneck Puerto Rican thrashing some caramel cutie with ten inches of uncut banana, entertained the quiet and mesmerized drunk. A Mandingo salad toss and then a ride on some cream-colored pony—boy trade was getting it and giving it every which way, tight and loose.

She continued to stare through those unblinking eyes, continued to eat popcorn, drink vodka, and gently probe her senior but still spit-moistable pussy.

But after she brought herself to a myriad of huckbucking climaxes, she felt vile, vile as vile's mother. Her drunkenness and her guilt were ill-mixed and she had sickened herself, was sick of herself, and hated herself all over again for the pain she had caused.

She remembered how sweet he was, how young he was, how fresh he was, how bright he was. If she had only remembered discipline.

But how could she have known? She was weakened by lust, wilted by proclivities she could not control. That is what she had told herself throughout the years, even if she had yet to convince herself. Time had not gauzed over the picture. The colors had not faded. The transgression still stood crystal clear, in spite of what she tried to tell herself.

Time.

Time does not make everyone forget. Time had not let Earl-Anthony forget, had not let his mother forget. A scalding is always remembered. So what happened more than twenty years ago felt as if it had happened just yesterday.

In theory Selma Fant was the near perfect mother for a homosexual son. Some mothers just come fit to order, others have to be dragged to it like gluttons to tofu. But Selma Fant was near perfect. She was girlfriend and guardian, both shield and mantle. She was near perfect except for that one mighty thing. It did not matter that what happened occurred so long ago, when Earl-Anthony was still living at home, was still her perfect little man, years before he became the diva Miss Zara. The pain suffered by both mother and child was a deep, rugged canyon not easily traversed.

Peter Caise.

Peter.

Peter Peter Pumpkin Eater. That's what she called him once she discovered all he could do.

More than twenty years ago. She had come home early, had shown all her listings and closed two escrows. She was feeling no pain when she came through the front door, went to the bar, and fixed a celebratory cocktail.

She almost snapped on the music when she recognized the huffing and puffing of Earl-Anthony working out in his room upstairs. She decided to share her good news with him.

She set down her drink and swept up the stairs like a schoolgirl home from a great night at the prom. She smiled to herself as she moved down the hallway; the midafternoon sun from their bay windows poured through Earl-Anthony's wide open bedroom door. And the strains and the grunts and the huffs and the puffs from her hardworking baby working harder than usual made her smile with pride at his sense of dedication to physical fitness, so unlike his potbellied, near-wasted daddy.

A pride-filled smile was still plastered on her face as she stood frozen one step inside his bedroom. Her eyes became bulges as she stared at the sight: the horror and the beauty, the anger and desire, the heart-beating pulse of the rhythm of the two bodies connected like yard dogs in heat. She was repelled and rekindled by how well her son was taking it and loving it, how well his friend was riding it and giving it. She was deeply moved and thoroughly disgusted. She shed a tear and almost let out with a "Bravo, you bitches!"

For she wanted it. She wanted to love it and taste it and take it as good as her son was.

Move over, son, and let Mommy get some!

And then she felt bad, guilty as hell; but before she could look away he looked up and saw her. And when he smiled that dangerous smile that knew that she wanted whatever it was he was giving her child, her guilty-as-hell went straight out the window.

So while Earl-Anthony Fant was getting it too good to open his eyes, his man and his mom were eyeing each other and planning with smiles that were guilty but not guilty enough.

Guilty-as-hell was long gone.

So she stayed at the door and she stared. And he gave her the show, a preview of things surely to come, a taste of the medicine she'd get for her cold. He even pulled out his fat, swollen dick that was grinding her son, throbbing revealingly through shimmering form-fitting latex, and with it he slapped her son's ass. She suddenly let out with the tiniest peep, which was hidden beneath the grunts and the grinds and the huffs and the puffs of her son begging it back inside where it belonged.

Sticky, damp, and overwhelmed, she then silently curled herself around the outside of her son's bedroom doorway and propped her throbbing body up against the hallway wall and grabbed at her heart, quick-beating underneath a stiff-nippled titty.

She then caught her breath, held it, and listened and listened and listened, and then sucked her thumb before running away.

Damn him. Damn him to hell. That motherfucking Peter. She cursed him the first time he fucked her, called him a low-down motherfucking son-of-a-bitch, and he totally agreed with her.

Then one day she yelled "motherfucker" too loudly, and

in classic what-goes-around-comes-around fashion, Earl-Anthony got home early enough to stand in the doorway and watch while his mother got fucked by his boyfriend.

And he wished for a gun. He wished that he could shoot him. Shoot him while he came, shoot him while he screamed at her, "Who's yo' mothafuckin' baby! Who's yo' mothafuckin' baby *now!*" Shoot him so his eyes would bulge and his jaws would drop and his blood and his sperm would splatter and splash all over his chest and all over her breasts. Shoot him so that he would fall dead on top of her. And then she could scream, "Bloody murder! Bloody murder!" and ask herself, Why? And then she could wonder until her last, dying day: *How could you do such an unholy thing, bringing all of this pain to your child?*

And then Selma looked up and saw her son, a zigzag blur of him. But Peter was bouncing and riding her blindly and wildly, and she could not think and she tried to make him stop with her fists while the walls of her pussy sided with pleasure.

Chapter Eleven

Peter was a real trip," Miss Zara mused. "He loved me, and hated the fact that he loved me . . . loved another man. So when Mother gave him that Mrs. Robinson wink he just knew that that would be the cure. Shit, fucking my mother made him more of a punk than he ever was, fucking me."

"So where's Peter now?" Brando asked.

"Last time I heard, he was dating a Detroit Piston."

"Oh yeah, I remember that."

"That had to be, what? Ten, twelve years ago?"

"Was it that long ago?"

"Yeah. You had just graduated from law school. Had moved back to Hancock Park with your parents."

"Right."

"I remember the first time you came down to the Queen Mary in the Valley to see me perform. Shocked the shit out of you."

"You didn't shock me."

"Don't lie."

"I just didn't know which was more beautiful, you as a man or you as a woman."

"Smooth." She laughed. "You lawyers always know what to say."

"But it's true, Zara." Brando looked at her, and still he could see the beautiful church boy who broke his heart deep down inside her, and yet, who she was this day was truly who she was meant to be. And she was beautiful.

"Why Peter and not me?" he suddenly asked.

"Aw, come on, Brando, that was a long time ago."

"I know, and I'm over it. But I just wanted to know. Why?"

"Why are you just now asking?"

"I don't know if I was ready to know until now. When I came home for summer break, I found out you had moved out of your parents' house, and no one knew where you were. Then I saw you down at the Horizon."

"The whore zone." She laughed at the bitter memory of her days anesthetizing her pain at the sleazy Washington Boulevard hole in the wall.

"Dancin' your ass off, high as a kite."

"Shakin' it off, baby. Shakin' it off."

"You hardly recognized me, Zara."

"I recognized you, baby boy. I just didn't want you to see me like that."

"You were so fucked up."

"I was, wasn't I?"

"And I wanted to know what could have done this to such a beautiful person."

"The Peters of the world. The mothers of the world."

"So why Peter and not me?"

"I was your teacher, Bran. You were the student. I still had things to learn that you couldn't teach me."

"You can always learn from a student."

"Not the bitter lessons I needed to know. I needed to learn how to hold hot coal and not flinch. I can do that now, and I'm sure now so can you."

When Selma finally emerged from her den, she could not believe the sky had now become iridescent and dark Rembrandt gold. The smoke from the fires in Malibu billowed apocalyptically skyward, crossing paths with the red-orange sun descending safely behind the sparkling Pacific horizon.

She turned her cell phone back on then went through the house and turned the ringers back on all of the landlines she had dismantled. She was a person of great dedication to whatever it was she was dedicated to at the moment, whether it was a cocktail or a fantasy. When she watched her videos she did not want the mood hindered or broken by some ring of a bell, ending the round while it was just getting good.

From high noon to sunset she had been busy in the dark with her videos and cocktails and stinging memories, and it did not occur to her that she had not seen or heard from her husband all day. All she knew was it was time to pull herself together. Clymenthia Teager's reading and signing was just two hours away and she had to look good for the gorgeous gay boys who would be there in droves.

Chapter Twelve

Eso Won Books was packed an hour before Clymenthia Teager was scheduled to read. After confirming with Omar his pre-reading interview with the author, Jeanette Bell mingled with the mass of early arrivals and joked charmingly with various members of the literary press and the early-arriving women of United Lesbians of African Heritage (ULOAH). She could see out of the corner of her eye the two men in the magazine section checking her out, particularly the one licking his lips like LL, demented, with hungry eyes scanning her up and down. She was used to it, yes, but still bothered by it, even to the point of paranoia.

She checked her watch, then signaled to Omar to give her ten minutes. She started toward the back of the store when one of the hungry-eyed men, Ramon Alexander, not heeding his buddy's gesture of caution, strutted toward her, cutting her off at the pass.

"May I help you?" she asked, meeting him eye to eye.

"So wassup with you?" Ramon asked her breasts.

"Your biggest nightmare," she answered, stepping around him.

Whipped by her jasmine scent, Ramon pivoted with a not-so-subtle pimp-daddy cool she knew would come next, but she did not break her stride. He winked at his buddy and caught back up with her.

"Oh I see," he assessed. "You know what your problem is, my sista? You just ain't met the right man yet."

"You know what your problem is, my brutha?" she responded. "Neither have you." She entered through the back storage room doorway, and shut it tightly behind her, causing Ramon to fume, which his friend Tyler Martin knew could only mean trouble.

Clymenthia, having just finished meditating, smiled at the sight of her beautiful partner coming toward her. Jeanette kissed Clymenthia gently on her smiling lips.

"Hey," Jeanette purred sexily, trying to mask the tenseness brought on by the encounter she had just had.

"Hey yourself," Clymenthia responded, noticing the strange look on Jeanette's face. "What's wrong, babe?" she asked.

"Nothing, sweetie," Jeanette said. "Just a little harassment from a damn breeder. Looking good out there," she said, changing the subject. "Almost as good as Philly. A lot of the sisters from ULOAH in the house."

"Good."

"They want you for their retreat next year. I told them yes. It'll coincide with the new book."

"Don't be so sure, baby."

"I'm *very* sure. The manuscript is in great shape, one of your best first drafts. Your editor's going to feel shamed for taking the company's money. Trust me."

"Thank you, baby," Clymenthia said with a grateful smile as Jeanette leaned in and kissed her again.

"Ready for Omar Stevens?"

"Sure, bring him in."

Chapter Thirteen

Selma Fant had barely sobered up but managed to maneuver the steep and winding drive down La Brea Avenue. She pulled into a parking space on the side of the bookstore and checked herself in the rearview mirror. Her eyes were a mess, red and veiny. She threw on her sunglasses though the night was midnight blue save for the sparkle of orange shooting up like earth-propelled lightning, a sign the fires in Malibu had not subsided.

She stepped from her car with a stumble. The handsome, honey-colored young Latino stepping out of the car parked next to hers asked if she was all right. "Fine, hon," she answered with a smile more solid than her walk. He smiled back at her in a sad, lovely way that reminded her of Earl-Anthony's sad, lovely smile. Shane then gestured her toward the door and held it for her, and she felt like Blanche DuBois with her paperboy.

As she entered past him, Shane stopped at the door for a moment and surveyed the room of handsomely dressed patrons and literary press. That's when he saw Thomas and

Andrew, the track runner and the Silver Lake thug prince. And that's when they saw him. They were near triplets, a triptych of Brando Heywood. They were tributes to all that seemed to be in Omar's longing, aching heart for Brando. Omar saw none of them, or pretended not to, as he was being led by Jeanette to the back room for his interview with Clymenthia Teager.

Shane stepped into the store just in time to see Omar disappear into the back room.

"You see him?" Senior Father purred out of nowhere. His lilac cologne purred as loudly.

"I saw him," Shane answered.

"You think he saw you?"

"I'm sure he didn't. He's focused on his interview."

"And you're here to unfocus him."

"No, not really. He's here doing his job, Senior Father. Afterward I want him to focus on me."

"Yes, well . . . now, don't forget. Two weeks from today. My winter supper."

"I won't."

"I hope you two are still together by then."

Senior Father Lacey Cannon delighted in drama. His instigation so casually set up earlier in church—an inevitable showdown between Shane and Omar—was about to be played out with a hyperbolic denouement worthy of pulp fiction. Shane never struck Senior Father as the violent type, but a swift, jealousy-induced ass whuppin' in the presence of L.A.'s distinguished black, same-gender-loving literary community would be the talk of the town, fodder for good cocktail conversation for his upcoming annual get-together.

But if the showdown was going to happen it was not going to happen now. Omar had disappeared into the back room. Shane continued to stare long at the closed door before aiming his gaze at the two other clones who were staring at him.

Chapter Fourteen

Dinner at Brando's parents' Hancock Park home had been a Sunday ritual for Brando and Collier when they were together. However, in the two years since the breakup, Mr. and Mrs. Heywood often filled Collier's vacancy with the most beautiful, intelligent, accomplished, and eligible women social standing could provide. Dee Dempsey-Bohannon, subtly pitched earlier at church, and this evening's chosen candidate, was no exception. During aperitifs Dee impressed all three Heywoods with her vast knowledge of Mayan art and its root connection to precolonial African culture. During dinner she praised Mrs. Heywood's southern Texas cuisine and cleaned her plate twice, in open defiance of her trim, fashion-model waist and physique. After dinner she and Mr. Heywood gleefully rummaged through his pristine collection of jazz 78's, and later she proved to be as adept at bid whist as she was at selling wolf tickets, leading the women's partnership to a 4-0 victory before the men begged off.

Brando then made his apologies, realizing it was almost time for the Clymenthia Teager signing and reading.

"Clymenthia Teager's reading tonight?" Dee's eyes widened.

"Yes," Brando answered. "You know her work?"

"Are you kidding me? I'm one of her biggest fans. I had no idea she was in town."

"She's a client of mine. The reading's at Eso Won. Would you like to join me?"

"I'd love to!"

Mr. and Mrs. Heywood nudged each other with gleeful anticipation as they bade the couple farewell.

"Dee, why don't you leave your car parked in our driveway and ride with Brando?" Mr. Heywood suggested slyly.

"Good idea, Pops," Brando enthused innocently. "Is that okay with you, Dee?"

"Great."

"You kids have a good time tonight," Mrs. Heywood urged hopefully, standing in the doorway with her husband of forty-three years.

"We will," the "kids" assured in unison as Brando held the passenger door open for his guest.

Brando's Mercedes glided effortlessly down Highland Avenue, headed south, past old world residences that hid and housed tastefully lush floral gardens, ancient but well-cared-for swimming pools, and quiet, old-family money. Brando's top was down and the warm evening breeze whipped gently through Dee's flawless hair.

Dee closed her eyes, leaned her head back, and savored the gardenia-scented breeze that caressed her perfect face.

"You do know what your parents are up to," she said without opening her eyes.

"It's a running thing with them." Brando sighed good-naturedly. "But it's okay. It's actually kind of sweet."

"I just got out of three years with a very nice but boring Neanderthal," Dee then said. "Right now I'm enjoying this new round of life-after-death of a marriage."

"I've been out of my relationship for two years. We were together for ten."

"Do your parents know you're gay?"

Brando was surprised.

"How did you know?" he asked.

"I kind of figured."

"Really?" Brando chuckled. "How'd you kind of figure?"

"Radar. Ego. Not that I was fishing, but when you look as good as I do, with these legs and breasts and face, a subtle checkout from the most discriminating gentleman is a given. You never looked beyond my eyes, not at church earlier, nor during a single moment at your parents'."

"Flirting in church?"

"Well, it is where most folks find the best pickings."

"Touché."

"So, do they know?"

"Yes, they do."

"Then why are they trying to set you up with me?"

"They still think it's a phase."

"How long have they known?"

"Since I was eighteen. Probably earlier."

"And how old are you now?"

"Forty."

"That's a helluva phase." She laughed.

"For them, hope springs eternal." He laughed as well.

"So you were in a relationship for ten years," she continued.

"Yep."

"That's pretty good."

"He was a good guy...is a good guy. We just grew apart."

"Well actually, so is my ex. I mean, I really should not have called him a Neanderthal," Dee confessed. "He's really a very nice man, a successful TV director who afforded me a wonderful lifestyle."

"So what happened?"

"Work. His work is everything to him, and this star is not used to playing a supporting role."

"I kind of figured."

"How did you kind of figure?"

"Radar. Ego. I know a diva when I see one."

And that's when she opened her eyes. She saw he was smiling. And so was she.

Chapter Fifteen

She wanted to be a writer the first time she read James Baldwin. She was mesmerized by his use of language, writing that expressed an extraordinary self-confidence.

She grew up with magnificent role models. She didn't fully understand that until she was older. The Southern black women in her life were extraordinary women for their time.

Although she and her life partner lived on a small farm in Connecticut, Atlanta would always be her home.

Her mother was the librarian at Spelman College. Her grandmother's family owned the hospital. Her other grandmother's family owned the local black newspaper. The family of a friend of her mother's owned the mortuary.

These were the women she grew up with. And what she also realized as she grew older was the extraordinary price that these women and their men paid to be free and black in the South.

Her father ran his own business. He was a contractor. But she didn't learn until she got older that he was a college graduate working on his master's and the only job he could get was either in the post office delivering mail or as a Pullman porter.

One day he said, "Well I'll be damn. I didn't put myself through school to serve white people on a train." So he made a business for himself.

This is who she wrote about, people who were proud of who and what they were, people who were self-confident. She wrote about her people, the people who made her who she was, the people who made her Clymenthia Teager.

Omar turned off the tape recorder.

Chapter Sixteen

Selma Fant's drunken high was beginning to wear off. She even managed to stand up straight when Brando escorted the beautiful female stranger into the store. The triptych perked up at the sight of him too, separately comparing themselves to him.

Selma smiled as bright as she could when Brando introduced her to Dee and she wondered, was this Dee just another fag hag claiming a piece of the spotlight gay men shed on their female compatriots? Or was she infallible pussy determined to convert the unconvertible, or at least get a charity taste of those lovely eight inches that Selma, through her own electronic means, secretly knew Brando had? Whoever, whatever she was, she was gorgeous; as gorgeous as Selma once was.

And Selma felt no malice or jealousy. She liked a lady who liked what she liked. And so Brando left them to chat while he checked on his client.

"So how'd the interview go?" he asked Omar, meeting him on his way out.

"Not one to brag, but when brilliant minds like ours confab, journalistic genius births forth."

"Yeah, uh-huh. You would want to birth forth something for the three musketeers"—Brando nodded discreetly—"daggering you over there in the corner."

He then abandoned his friend to the wolves.

Omar smiled at the triptych weakly. His smile was not returned as they each waited to see to whom the wind would blow him. He decided to play it safe by first placating the most lethal of the three. Shane. He smiled apologetically at Shane and urged him over.

"Hey, baby."

"You ain't shit, you know that?"

"What?"

"You just don't have any consideration for my feelings, do you?"

"Aw, baby, now you know that ain't true."

"Which one of them did you fuck while I was in church this morning, you heathen mothafucka?"

"Come on, baby, how you gonna talk about church—"

"Like yo' ass give a flyin' fuck."

"—and use that kinda language all in the same sentence?"

"The same way I can hate you and love you all in the same sentence."

"Really?"

"Don't even."

"Hey . . . co . . . come on . . . look," Omar stuttered. "This isn't really the place to get into all of this."

"Then when and where, Omar?"

"Later. Afterward."

"Do I need to take a number?"

"Aw, you gone really play me like that, huh?"

"Naw, Negro, you done already played *yourself*."

The track runner and the Silver Lake thug prince were shaking their heads in unison, dual but distant witnesses to the bullshit they knew so well. They had gotten pretty friendly over the course of the evening, and the friendliness appeared to evolve into a conspiracy from Omar's vantage point.

Omar knew he damn well better stay attentive to Shane, yet he could not help but notice what was going on behind Shane's back. And what was going on was beginning to make him sweat just a bit. After all, neither the track runner nor the Silver Lake thug prince had much to lose. They both got theirs earlier and they could tell that the muted read-down Omar was getting came from someone who had not gotten his share.

"And don't be fuckin' lookin' at them when I'm fuckin' talkin' to yo' ass!"

"Huh?"

"You wanna be with them, or you wanna be with me?"

"I wanna be with you, Shane, you know that. But sometimes I wanna be with them. And you know that, too."

"So what are we anyway?"

"Boyfriends."

"Look, I ain't in no damn high school lookin' to go to the fuckin' prom. I need more than a boyfriend, Omar. I need a committed partner and some exclusivity."

"I thought we already settled that."

"*You* settled it."

"And you agreed. Hey, I thought we were going to talk about this later."

"What time are you getting home?"

"Gimme a couple hours. I promised Brando I'd meet him and the ladies for a drink afterward."

"Why can't I come along?"

"Because we'll be drinking."

"You and Brando fucking?"

"What do you think?"

"I'm thinkin' you wishin' the answer was yes."

"Don't go there. Come by around midnight."

"I'll be there. And *you* be there."

"You know how much I love making love to you when you're pissed?"

"You know how much you still ain't shit? Sorry-ass mothafucka. Midnight!"

Shane turned and walked away. Omar felt his dick growing down his leg at the very sight of the firm high-hoisted ass in sheer linen slacks disappearing down the nonfiction aisle and out the front door. "Mm-mm-mm," Omar muttered, shaking his head and licking his lips. Only the scent of the clashing colognes let him know what was coming up behind him.

"Hey, fellas," he said with a debonair smile as he turned to face them. "Wassup?"

Chapter Seventeen

Jeanette Bell and Brando Heywood had met three years earlier when they both shared the dais at the Economic Empowerment Summit held during the D.C. Black Lesbian and Gay Pride Celebration. They became good friends and mutual admirers quickly. The fact that they were both in committed relationships gave them much to talk about and welcome comfort as they were both in D.C. away from and missing their respective partners. How Jeanette spoke of Clymenthia was inspiring and revealing. Brando secretly envied the intensity of a relationship he knew he did not experience—a relationship, perhaps, he was incapable of experiencing. If only he could have loved Collier with the passion it was quite clear Jeanette had for Clymenthia, an obvious gushing even underneath Jeanette's no-nonsense Condoleezza Rice demeanor and Gabrielle Union beauty.

"Come on, baby, it's time," Jeanette whispered to Clymenthia with a soft gentle kiss as Brando looked on, his hands in his pockets, absently jangling loose change.

Oh to be kissed with a kiss like that kiss.

"So how do I look?" Clymenthia asked Brando, caught off guard daydreaming.

"Like a literary celebrity in love," he answered with a slight smile. "You two really make me miss Collier," he added without thinking.

"And whose fault is that?" Jeanette responded softly, holding open the door that let in the harsh neon light and loud cheers and applause.

Chapter Eighteen

...*t* his time of year the fog hovers thickest over that part of the ocean that meets the shore. It is where she walks this time of year. But mist cannot hide her. And that is just fine. She has nothing to hide. It is here where the natives embrace winter solstice.

"The chill and the salt and spray teasers. They do not disturb her. They love her.

"She is black. Blue-black and mellow. Lady panther in Eden. At home on the range with the sheep and the lamb. Partnered in paradise.

"She is gold. Precious. Strong-willed and soft-spoken. Naively clever. A wickedly schoolgirlish woman.

"She sells notions and lotions and things healthy and clean at the small seaside shop off the breeze. Not in love at the moment, except with the world, with the wind, with herself, but she knows that one day she will gleefully fall. For as good as all things are, the best comes yet. That is why she always smiles that smile.

"So in the meantime, in the sweet time, she will walk along

the beach, disappear into the fog that does not hide her, and she will find the waves and play them."

Answers seemed to exist all around Brando. And as he listened to Clymenthia's words, words he had heard so many times, had read so many times, he still could not grasp what he needed to make sense of his life. Patience, perhaps. Was he too anxious for love, too anxious to experience that feeling he once felt so long ago? Had he been so devastated by that life-changing experience with Earl-Anthony that now his emotions were too tightly confined beneath the armor he so desperately wanted to discard, tear from, singe off, but did not have madness enough to do so?

He wanted to be undignified enough to scream bloody murder, or at least as free and as hopeful as Clymenthia's protagonist, walking through the mist with her head held high and her heart opened to the infinite possibilities of love that most assuredly would come . . . someday. If only he could make himself believe.

As Clymenthia continued, on occasion peering over her reading glasses to smile with her crowd, Brando, standing next to Dee, caught sight of Omar's track runner and Silver Lake thug prince, two men who had passionate eyes for his passionate friend. *What is that like? What is the Godness of it all? Why can't I feel like that? Why do I have all of the questions but none of the answers, none of the feelings that should come with the quest?*

And then he felt Dee take his hand and squeeze it ever so gently. And the squeeze caught him off guard, and he flinched ever so slightly. And when their eyes met, he knew that she knew and that she understood, somehow. The platonic affection that flowed from her palm through his was at least a small comforting sign that all was not lost and that perhaps hope was not a futile thing.

The evening had been a roaring success for Clymenthia. The lover and the lawyer and the writer and the crowd, willful and gleeful collaborators on the success of the event, applauded their star and themselves. Teager's new book flew off the shelves and she greeted and signed tirelessly for two straight hours. She gave each of her fans attention one would seemingly give to an only fan. She signed something different and personal in each book of hers offered.

But every few minutes or so she would look past her fans, for a moment or two, and search out the proud, smiling face of the woman she loved. More than anything else, that made it all worthwhile.

Clymenthia Teager, however, was not the only one eyeing Jeanette Bell. With an intensity that scared even his friend, Ramon Alexander stared at the lesbian beauty. And his stare bore into her with such intensity that Tyler, his friend, whispered to him with cautious cool, "You wanna be messin' up like this?"

"No, uh-uh," Ramon growled back quietly. "Ain't no fuckin' dyke dissin' me like that. Fuck that shit."

And so Tyler shook his head and threw up his hands and started out the door, knowing too well how Ramon could be.

Chapter Nineteen

Brando, Dee, Omar, Jeanette, and Clymenthia caravanned up to the La Brea summit and down Overhill Drive, just past Slauson Avenue, to La Louisianne for drinks and a late-night snack. Like actors jazzed after a triumphant performance, they toasted and munched on crab cakes and salmon bites and laughed loudly in a soul-plush establishment that welcomed the robust. Brando had arranged for a congratulatory cake to be brought to their table and the house band performed a special arrangement of Stevie Wonder's "Overjoyed" in honor of the novelist. Jeanette beamed uncharacteristically schoolgirlish and when the band ended its tribute with a fanfare, she reached over and kissed her woman so passionately that the house—gay, straight, and bi—had to give it up like tarry-service holy rollers.

Omar was unusually quiet as he watched the two female lovebirds, and wondered why he treated Shane so badly. The sin that sin begot, that's what his mother used to call him, and maybe that's what he believed about himself. But maybe it was time to stop giving the woman who begrudgingly gave him birth the power to damn him and burden him with self-fulfilling prophecy.

He missed his Grammy. He missed her love. He missed love. Grammy was gone and Brando was seemingly out of his reach. But he had a chance. All those other guys just got his dick hard and his rocks off. Shane made his heart flutter. He accepted that, and at this moment, seeing what true love was in the eyes of Jeanette and Clymenthia, wanted a little taste of that himself.

A committed, monogamous relationship. That's what Shane wanted. Would that be so hard? There was only one way to find out.

It was ten to twelve when Omar said his good-byes. He lived in Ladera Heights, only five minutes away, and he was truly feeling glad about seeing Shane. Brando gave him the thumbs-up and Omar appreciated the gesture. Maybe he should give Shane more of a chance, Omar thought to himself as he retrieved his car from the parking lot attendant. Maybe he should give himself more of a chance.

Back in the club the party wound down slowly. The three beautiful women and their handsome male crony ordered one more round and then coffee. Dee was in seventh heaven, having been made to feel like an old friend in this tight circle of friends that just so happened to include one of her favorite authors. Even earlier, hitting it off so well with the delightful if tipsy Selma Fant (they promised to get together for lunch later in the week), she knew that this evening would be special. She felt gleefully beholden to her new friend Brando, who already felt like a brother, and let him know with a smile. Why had she stayed so long from the fair?

But if she could only have known how grateful Brando was for her friendship, the friendship of all the women he knew and loved in his life, women who seemed to know about love in all of its stages—how committed and romantic Jeanette and Clymenthia truly were, Dee's fond and passionate memories of a good, loving man who probably lost out because he worked too hard to give her everything, and his own mother, who glowed with the time-tested love of his father.

And so it was moments like these, friends like these—even Omar—who would prop up Brando's teetering faith, who would somehow protect him from sinking into the frigid waters of total cynicism and emotional sterility.

The band's singer, a big, buxom, dark chocolate beauty, closed the last set with a rousing version of "Here's to Life," and the whole house agreed with an ovation that thundered.

The four then got up and made their way through the cordial crowd. As they neared the door, neither of the four noticed the single pair of eyes in the dark that followed them, coldly monitoring their every move.

Shane was parked in front of Omar's town house when Omar drove into the driveway. By the time Omar had gotten out of his car Shane was standing in front of him.

"Been here long?" Omar asked, noticing how the moonlight sparkled in Shane's beautiful dark brown eyes.

"About ten minutes," Shane answered flatly.

"Sorry I'm late."

"You're not late, just sorry."

"See? You're starting already."

"You're right." Shane's eyes glazed. "I'm sorry."

"No you're not," Omar said softly, sweetly. "You're anything but." He looked deep into Shane's questioning eyes and gave him a small reassuring smile. Shane wasn't quite sure what to make of it. Dare he get his hopes up? Could it be that Omar was changing? He did not want to think about it too much. The moment existed for him to enjoy. The night lay ahead for both of them.

Without another word Omar went to his front door, unlocked it, and opened it. He turned back to Shane, who had silently followed him. Omar's eyes were the invitation Shane cautiously accepted. He entered past Omar, who then entered and closed the door behind them.

In the dark of the foyer, streaked by a single ray of moonlight, the kiss was so soft and unhurried that it captured the single tear Shane could no longer hold back. He could no longer hold back much of anything now. He surrendered and began to sob. And Omar let him know that it was okay. He held Shane in his arms and laid his head on his chest. Then he shed tears of his own. And for the moment he forgot about Brando.

"God, how I love Sundays," Dee said as she and Brando sat in Brando's car in front of his parents' house.

"Me, too."

"Thanks, Brando. Tonight was the perfect topper."

"I'm glad you came along."

"Your ex didn't know what he had."

"Neither did yours."

"You know, it really wasn't his fault."

"Same here."

"Sounds like we got a whole lot in common, sister girl."

"Sounds that way, don't it?" Dee laughed thoughtfully.

She and Brando sat in the car basking in the spotlight of the moon.

"I'm glad your parents tried to set us up." Dee smiled. She closed her eyes, gently threw her head back, and ran her fingers through her soft, wind-tussled hair.

"So am I," Brando said, kissing her softly on the cheek. They both knew it without saying it. They felt like the sibling that neither had.

Chapter Twenty

He followed Jeanette Bell and Clymenthia Teager over the hill and then west on the 10 freeway. Their rental car bore his mark just in case, a broken right-side taillight cover.

At Robertson Boulevard the naked light signaled and he followed them off and then left to the beautifully appointed Culver City hotel. He parked on the opposite side of the street and watched as they pulled into the hotel's open-air parking lot, a sprawling front lawn of black tarmac and white strips barely lit under tall neon lamps sentried vast distances apart. Few other cars occupied slots.

The two women, wearied by a day of preparation, presentation, and celebration, stepped out of the car and met on the driver's side.

"Fuckin' dyke bitches," he mumbled to himself as he watched them, watched her, ever-so-ladylike, lock the door to the car and place the keys in her purse.

"Naw," he said louder this time but still to himself, shaking his head, when she leaned in and kissed her girl like her girl was some fuckin'-ass dude.

They headed toward the hotel and the echo infuriated him.

The other one had on tennis shoes; the big one, the man one, the writer. But the main one, the bitch with the attitude, she had on heels like she was fooling somebody.

But he truly knew better and so did his heart. His heart beat in step with each click of her heels and his sweaty palms strangled the steering wheel he sat rigidly behind. Though his car's engine idled smoothly, his heart and his mind were agitated and indignant. Anger and lust dangerously commingled.

He willed her to stop and face her comeuppance. And she did. They did.

The first fuckin' dyke bitch touched the other one's arm. She then said something to her and the other one nodded. Then the clicking heels with the attitude clicked back toward the car they had left and he knew it was now, man, or never.

His sweating hands steered the car into an easy U-turn. The car entered the street entrance of the hotel's guest parking lot. The one fuckin' dyke bitch unlocked the car while the other stood in the entrance of the hotel and smiled a longing dyke smile. But he knew it would do her no fuckin' dyke good.

The smell of the smoke in the air drew Clymenthia's attention upward and she remembered. The fires in Malibu were still out of hand. She said a silent prayer for the beach community and thanked her lucky stars for all that had been given to her.

And then she looked over.

"Come on, baby, what's taking you so long?" she mumbled to herself, suddenly realizing how bad she had to pee. Jeanette was a stickler and Clymenthia loved her for that, but when you gotta go, you gotta go. The notes Jeanette went back to the car to get didn't need to be read in the car.

"Read 'em in the room, baby, read 'em in the room."

With a sigh Jeanette was more than familiar with, Clymenthia started across the lot briskly, squeezing her thighs tightly with every quick step.

As she got closer to the car she could see that Jeanette was not inside and nowhere to be found. She wondered out loud, "How the hell did she get past me?"

She hightailed it back to the hotel lobby and found the ladies' lounge. She knew she would never have made it up to the room.

What she did not know was that in a previous half moment a man set on vengeance and payback for crimes uncommitted had pulled up next to Jeanette, dazed her with a single blow, dragged her into his car, and disappeared into a night that would witness the evil some men do.

Chapter Twenty-one

Jeanette Bell awoke with that short heaving that comes with the terror of not knowing what is happening, yet knowing that whatever it is, it is wrong. She was bent over the hood of a gray Nissan Altima, her hands bound before her by the strap of her purse that she clutched tightly with each brutal plunge.

His hand quickly covered her mouth and her nose when she tried to scream, and she could hardly breathe, but he did not care. He cursed at her and laughed viciously as he slammed into her like a battering ram over and over and over until her rectum bled.

Through all of the pain she bit at his hand, wrestled back and forth, struggled up and down, straddled on the hood, fought on her stomach, slammed the back of her head in his face, but against the 260-pound sex-maddened animal, it was futile. He delighted in the pain that his ten inches gave her and when he finally came he howled and shivered and rammed her with a violence that bruised her ribs.

Spent, satisfied, and exhausted, he fell on top of her. The impact sent a sharp shivering pain through her chest.

He finally got up off her. Then he grabbed her by the hair

and flung her to the ground. She was too injured to scream out, though the pain demanded it, even as she rolled in the rocky dirt, her hands still bound together by the strap of her purse.

He looked over at her and laughed as he rolled the cum-filled, blood-and-excrement-covered condom down his still-dripping dick. He then threw it at her.

"Now I'm *yo'* biggeth nightmare, bith!" he growled with a lisp like a school-yard bully as he pulled his pants up and zipped them, never taking his eyes off the battered and disheveled woman heaped like a discarded rag doll on the ground before him, torn clothes everywhere.

He then wiped at his brow and shook his bald head at the battle he had barely won. He didn't really want to, or so he told himself, but he had to beat her while he fucked her because she fought back so fiercely. Fought like a banshee. And when he finished with her he was huffing and puffing like he'd just gone ten rounds.

He then shook his bald head and felt for his ten inches, making sure that they were still there.

And then for the first time he noticed the salty taste in his mouth and the whistling breeze through the new gap in his mouth that created the lisp. He dabbed at his mouth gingerly and felt the fresh snaggletooth, then looked down at his fingers and saw the blood.

"You fuckin' raggedy-atth bith!" He growled at her sprawled on the ground. "You knocked out my fuckin' teeff!" His eyes burned into her as he advanced with his bloody fist balled.

Desperately she scooted away, kicking dust in his path.

"Oh, yo gone get yo' atth whupped now."

And just as he reached her, a cloud of dust between them, he saw the flash and heard the blast that caught him in the shoulder and spun him around. The rat-tat-tat-tat-tat then stung each of his ass cheeks, and exploded his ball sacks. Five distinct pops danced his hell-destined torso round in a minstrelsy circle of unbearable pain until he grimaced and was facing the woman he'd raped, her purse in one hand and a small-caliber pistol smoking in the other. His eyes bulged like Buju Banton getting fucked by rough dick for the first declared time. Through the shock and pain he caught sight of the vengeance in her unblinking eyes. Then he caught sight of that final squeeze of the trigger as his whole miserable life flashed before him.

And the last thing he swore that he saw was the bullet coming right at his face. The last thing he swore that he felt was the explosion in his forehead that crossed his eyes and froze them in place as he fell to his suddenly manless man knees, as if hastened to a piteous punk prayer before smashing facedown in the dirt that engulfed his stank brandy-soaked corpse in a billow of dust.

Jeanette was so angry she shivered. She threw up and created a puddle of vomit and blood. Some poured down her neck. She wiped at the smear with maddening defiance.

And then for the first time that night she cried.

Part Two

Chapter Twenty-two

Early-morning joggers discovered the body of Ramon Jesse Alexander in a remote clearing across the street from Sony Pictures Studios. Culver City Police detective Edetta Franklin had gone over the crime scene thoroughly. Three days later the forensics report was on her desk. The blood on the discarded condom found at the scene—a condom that contained the victim's semen—was determined to be that of a woman. Heel marks in the dirt concurred. The amount of blood mixed with vaginal and anal secretions suggested trauma. The puddle of blood and vomit was further evidence. Trauma suggested rape, rape valiantly fought against. The tooth on the ground and the victim's fresh snaggletooth made the detective tense with an anger and pride of her own. "Right on, girl," she muttered under her breath, believing the rape victim fought strong and hard before likely and righteously blowing her rapist's brains out.

The interview with the dead victim's wife certainly lent credence to the victim's brutal aggressiveness with women. Charlene Alexander was stunned by the news. Detective Franklin noticed the bruises on Mrs. Alexander's face, and suspected spousal abuse. Mrs. Alexander's strange mixture of sorrow and relief was enough to arouse suspicion, but the fact that she was at a midnight tarry service, corroborated by her minister and fellow congregants, at the time the coroner determined her husband was killed spared her the accusatory finger.

Mrs. Alexander informed Detective Franklin that the last time she saw her husband was when he left with his running buddy, Tyler Martin, for the race track.

There was no love lost between Tyler Martin and Charlene Alexander. Ramon was the rope they tugged in opposite directions, both knowing they were attracted and repelled by Ramon, both masochists in love.

The next day Detective Franklin interrogated a clueless Tyler Martin, shocking him with the news Charlene Alexander did not bother informing him of. He was shocked and saddened, but not grief-stricken.

In fact he felt a morose relief. Since their days in the service together, as marines in the Gulf War, Tyler had always had a sexual attraction to Ramon that he fought hard to successfully mask. And he hated himself for the feelings he had—feelings when sharing the open shower in the middle of the desert, feelings when Ramon masturbated relentlessly to *Playboy* and pinups in the pup tent they shared, when Ramon gave him those tight brotha man hugs. It didn't help matters that Ramon had saved his life during a massive mortar attack. Tyler would forever be beholden to the war hero who turned him on to the point of distraction.

But now it was over: befriending a sexy sociopath who had no other friends, trying to repay an unpayable debt to an asshole, aching desires for someone who brought such pain and misery to so many.

It was over. It was a strange relief.

"How'd it happen?" Tyler asked the detective flatly.

"What time did you two leave Hollywood Park?" Detective Franklin asked, ignoring his question.

"Four, four-thirty. Somewhere around that. Right after the fourth race."

"And from there?"

"We stopped at the Living Room over on Adams and Crenshaw. Had a few drinks."

"Then?"

"We ended up over on La Brea. We see all these people going into Eso Won, so it's like all these fine women, so we pull up and go in, and they're having this book signing for some bull dag—"

Detective Franklin's pen stopped, but she didn't look up. Tyler caught himself. He proceeded cautiously.

". . . ah, so, like, we go in, and after awhile, he starts hittin' on this sista that ain't feelin' him, 'cause, you know, she's, well, you know, not feeling him."

"Go on."

"So, like, we hang there for a while. Then, after it's over, I leave."

"Alone."

"Yes."

"You and Mr. Alexander didn't leave together?"

"No."

"But you were riding together."

"I needed to get outta there."

"What do you mean?"

"Things were gettin' tense. Ramon was like gettin' into his thing and I didn't wanna be around when the explosion happened. I mean, he can be a kinda not-nice person—well I guess not anymore, huh? So I hopped on a bus."

"What do you mean about the explosion, him not being a nice person?"

"Ramon was never used to women telling him no. He didn't care if they was gay or not."

"About this woman he was hitting on. Do you remember anything about her?"

"Yeah, sure. I mean, she was like fine as all git-out, but hard, not hard *lookin'*, but attitude-wise; definitely a hater when it comes to the brothas. And it was obvious that she and the sista who was reading had a thing going on."

"What makes you think that?"

"The way they looked at each other, like a dude and his woman look at each other."

Chapter Twenty-three

There was a characteristic chill in the San Francisco mid-morning air, but Jeanette Bell, aching from her injuries and slow-bourgeoning guilt-laced anger, was warmed by Clymenthia's reassurance and love.

"Baby, he got exactly what he deserved," Clymenthia said to her again, with a bedtime-story kind of soothing. "If I had been there, I would have done worse. Or better."

In their suite at the Mark Hopkins Hotel, they dressed quietly and slowly for the reading and signing at A Different Light Bookstore in the city's Castro district. The night before, Clymenthia had read and signed at Marcus Books in Oakland. The evening before that, signings and readings in La Jolla and Sacramento brought out hundreds of Teager fans. Despite Clymenthia's protests and desire to end the tour, Jeanette would not allow the devastating events in Culver City to interfere with the last swing of the tour.

Dr. Eleanor Jamison, the physician Jeanette and Clymenthia sought down in L.A. the day after the rape, had been shocked by the bruised rib and facial and anal abrasions as she conducted her examination.

"What happened, Jeanette?" the doctor asked without looking up from her probe.

"It was just one of those things that got out of hand."

The doctor said little more, but surmised all too well what had happened. "You should report this," she finally suggested.

"There's nothing to report except a wild night that got out of hand."

"With a man."

"With a man."

Dr. Jamison had cleaned Jeanette's wounds and had given her a prescription for pain, along with a final gentle plea.

"Don't let this go, Jeanette."

If only the doctor could have known. It had not been let go. It had been dealt with.

Chapter Twenty-four

Dee Dempsey-Bohannon felt blessed and cursed. Life really had been very good to her, but she longed for more. She was still trying to convince herself that divorcing Kevin was the right thing to do, although no better man could be found or desired. But she had not been brought up to settle. This was the affinity she shared with her favorite writer, Clymenthia Teager. Settling was not an option.

Settling for a long-distance marriage was not an option.

That morning she had received a call from Kevin, who was shooting a Lifetime TV movie in Toronto. He missed the sound of her voice and just wanted to check up on her, make sure she was all right. Kevin was always just a phone call a way. That was the problem. One of the television industry's few A-list black directors, Kevin Bohannon spent more time on location than at home. He worked hard to give Dee a good material life, even as his hard work often deprived her of his physical affection.

But no matter where he was, Kevin always managed to call Dee every day when he was away.

Still, that wasn't good enough for Dee. In the beginning

she found herself hanging out with the other desperate Hollywood wives, who substituted their absentee husbands with Beverly Hills shopping sprees, Palm Springs spa visits, designer drugs, too much booze, pool boys, and tennis pros. The shopping sprees and husbandless spa trips began to bore her; she was too health-conscious and looks-conscious for anything more than the occasional drink. And drugs, like infidelity, were simply not her thing. Lovemaking with Kevin had spoiled her. She missed that almost as much as she missed his caring smile, his loving-kindness, and his manly gentleness.

On more than one occasion she wondered why the hell she discarded such a good man. And then she thought about who she was and what she believed. She did not settle.

How ironic that she had begun a friendship and was spending the afternoon with a woman who had clearly settled.

"He's got some little bimbo bitch on the side," Selma Fant groused as she swaggered toward her bar with their empty glasses, "which is just fine with me. The councilman and I haven't made love in years."

"No more for me, Selma," Dee protested. Selma ignored the protest and prepared two doubles.

The doorbell rang and Selma was in no shape to make the long and winding trek out of the family room, past the library, through the living room and foyer, to the front door.

"Want me to get that?"

"Would you, hon?"

"Sure."

"Thanks." Selma saluted her as she half drained her fresh glass.

Just as Dee entered the foyer the doorbell rang again and

she could see through the door's glass window two police officers, who, when she opened the door, removed their hats.

"Mrs. Fant?" the shorter one asked. The taller one stood
silent, trying his best not to look down at the ground.

"Ah, no, Officer, she's in the back," Dee said with a touch
of concern. "I'm a friend. Is there anything I can help you
with?"

"Actually, ma'am, I need to speak with Mrs. Fant."

"Please, come in," Dee responded, ushering them in, closing the door behind them. Concern was poorly masked in her
voice. "Right this way."

She led them through the house into the family room,
where Selma was smiling at her empty glass.

"Selma?" Dee alerted her gently. "These officers need to
speak with you."

Selma looked up and saw the two handsome men, stunning in their crisp black uniforms and their gold and silver
badges.

"Gentlemen," she declared with a proud and slushy grin,
"how may I help you?"

"Mrs. Fant," the short one began with hesitation in his
voice, "I'm afraid I have bad news." The proud slushy grin
froze on Selma Fant's face.

"It's your husband, Mrs. Fant . . ."

Slowly her glassy eyes stretched wide and the grin went
grotesque. Her hands were now trembling as she reached back
with one. And what Selma now knew was what Dee now
knew. Dee took her friend's trembling hand firmly. And as Selma's body began to tremble as well, Dee brought Selma into
her embrace; held her up, for she had weakened and could not

stand up on her own. The trembling erupted into near-violent shaking. Tears burst from the Norma Desmond–stretched eyes and something low and foreboding rumbled out from the now grotesque grin.

"I'm so sorry, ma'am," the short officer said as Selma wailed in Dee's arms.

The Malibu fires had raged nonstop for four days. Palatial homes deep in the hilltop bush had been completely consumed while dumbfounded wildlife succumbed cruelly to smoke and flames. When the fires were finally contained and workers were able to go in and assess the damage, their worst fears were realized. Human life had been lost as well. The number was thirteen and counting. Councilman Felton G. Fant and his girl-friend were two of them.

Chapter Twenty-five

All of Los Angeles was buzzing with the news of the councilman's death; he had been found in a smoldering Malibu ranch house, incinerated in the arms of his eighteen-year-old paramour.

It was the day after his funeral. Sunday. Preachers in churches all throughout the city spoke with a tear and a twinkle in their eye of his good deeds, great service, and how much he would be missed.

They also spoke of moral lessons to be learned from the dearly departed's illicit behavior. But they spoke carefully, so as not to self-incriminate. The snickered jokes were already overfilled with torrid truths applicable to them all.

Scandalous as it was, however, it was not scandalous enough to diminish the outpouring of love and affection the city unleashed in honor of the man. His popularity was legendary. He was right up there with other L.A.-bred political beloveds: Maxine Waters, Tom Bradley, the first Jimmy Hahn.

And for those not in the know, which would be anyone who was not at the invitation-only farewell, Selma Fant's drunken state (on the arm of her newest best girlfriend, Dee) was not a state of mourning, though she indeed mourned. Her drunken state was her general state. She relied on her liquor as she relied on her videos.

Miss Zara, clinging tightly to Eli, had come to the Saturday-afternoon service late and sat in the back of the crowded church where she had sung long ago as the young Earl-Anthony. She later trailed the procession to the cemetery, and left immediately after the interment. She did not want her mother to see her. Sorrow and guilt and the booze Selma guzzled in between sobs and fallouts would have been too close to a lethal combination, and as estranged as Miss Zara was from her mother, she did not wish her ill, especially now. Brando watched Miss Zara make her clean getaway. In fact, they saw each other. She gave him the look that comes from a longtime friend who understands. And he did.

There was no planned gathering at the widow's house after the burial. Tradition or not, many agreed that it was something Selma Fant would not be able to handle. The decision created great consternation among the orthodox and the press.

Selma did, however, invite Dee over for post-funeral cocktails.

Brando was glad Selma and Dee hit it off. He also recognized a ladies-only summit as it was being planned and resisted the urge to invite himself.

For him, there would be no hanging out in Hancock Park with his folks either. They had left immediately after the funeral for their Palm Springs time share. And now that Omar and Shane had gotten closer, more committed, Brando was beginning to miss his weekday happy hour hangouts with Omar. And there had been no hitting the club the Saturday night of the funeral, no him and Omar gleefully dancing their fortysomething-year-old asses off, the oldest couple on the dance floor. Omar had spent Saturday, day and night, with Shane on Catalina Island. But Omar had assured Brando he would be back in time for brunch at Lucy Florence. Certain things love and lust cannot get in the way of.

Things were changing for Omar. Brando was happy for him, although that tinge of jealousy he felt threw him for a tiny loop.

Brando spent the night alone, ordered in from Pizza Hut, dined with pay-per-view, soaked in a warm tub, and slept soundly.

The next morning, Sunday, he woke up at his usual 6:30 AM. What confused and surprised him was the dream he immediately remembered. It was a very sweet dream about Collier. Or was it Omar?

Chapter Twenty-six

"Shane is a whole new experience for me," Omar confessed to Brando as one of the twins served coffee and sweet potato pie. "This making love thing. I haven't made love since the nineties. Just sex. But making love? Wow. You know the first thing I want to do when I see him?"

"What?"

"Kiss him."

"What's wrong with that?"

"No, I mean really kiss him. That gentle shit."

"Good for you, Omar."

"Yeah," Omar agreed, perplexed. "I'm having a good time with him. He's really a pretty decent brotha. Did you know he doesn't drink or do drugs at all?"

"A lot of people don't."

"He's an alcoholic."

"Okay."

"The least little thing can set him off. Out at Catalina I ordered sparkling cider for him but I had to have my usual."

"Who's the alcoholic?"

"He was watching me drink and he was freaking out."

"But, Omar, that's serious for them."

"I know it is. He's been sober three years. When I know I'm going to see him I usually put the shit away. But bottom line? I like having my cocktail and getting high every once in a while, and I have no intention of giving it up."

And then he thought about it. "I guess I really should adjust when he's around, huh?" he asked softly.

"You like him, don't you?"

"I think so."

"Naw, you *really* like him."

"He aiight."

"I mean, I'm listening to you and I'm convinced. You *can* teach an old dog new tricks."

Omar considered what Brando said, and felt a certain guilt about the circumstance he was now in. Shane was more than a new trick, yet Omar still felt like the same old dog.

"Last night out at Catalina," he began out of nowhere, "we had this room that was tucked up in the hills, overlooking the ocean, full moon and everything, the whole nine yards, and he mentions—what's the word?"

"Love?"

"No, fool. Monogamy. Now I don't like that word any more than I like the L-word, but he brought it up. And when he said it, I started squirming like crazy. I felt the sweat coming on. But somehow I squirmed out of it. See, I don't think I'm ready for that, and I resent the fact that he made the offer. I've only been seeing him for like five weeks. How dare he rush me like that?"

"Omar, Omar. Why are you resentful?"

"I don't want to be put in that position."

"Okay, that's fine. But he's an individual. He wants what he wants and you want what you want. If you two don't want the same thing, it's not a matter of resentment. He hasn't done anything wrong by expressing his feelings. Instead of resenting him for expressing his feelings, why not just tell him, 'Hey, I respect your feelings but I'm not into that'?"

"Yeah, but if I say that, he might move on."

"He hasn't moved on yet and you haven't given him anything."

"I think I have."

"You've given him no commitment."

"I'm just not ready. I keep saying to myself that maybe when I get older, but if I get much older I'll be dead."

"Please."

"I know I'm going to get older, but somehow I don't think I'm going to get any more mature."

"Omar, let me tell you something. You got yourself a nice guy in Shane. You should be happy. Kick back and enjoy. Enjoy it for what it is. You sit back talking about 'Damn, I spent all those years worrying about the shit, when I could have spent all those years enjoying it.' You obviously like the guy. I've never heard you talk about anybody like you talk about Shane."

"You think so?"

"I think so."

"I wonder if I deserve him."

"Why not? Other than being a total ho', you ain't so bad."

"You really think so?"

"Yeah, I do."

"Really?"

"Really."

The moment of silence that followed should have been uncomfortable. It was not. They were even able to look into each other's eyes with something beyond friendship and feel no immediate shame. It was not until the moment that followed that they were shaken from this hypnotic state. The distant sound of the Sunday ritual drums a block away in Leimert Park had begun right on time, and the low muffled sounds that seemed so far away made their own silence conspicuous and their shared stare obvious and self-conscious.

"You know, I did something really bad when we were out at Catalina," Omar confessed slowly.

"What?"

"I called him out of his name."

"What?"

"Huh?"

"What did you call him?"

"You don't want to know."

Eyeing Brando from across the room, Vanessa Ellerbee could not tell what was being said to him, but his listening eyes said much. His attentiveness, his empathy, was so blessedly apparent. And now, as she sat there alone—William did not come home last night—she was thoroughly convinced. She would have to make her move.

Chapter Twenty-seven

Selma and Councilman Felton G. Fant had grown apart years ago. Appearances were meticulously maintained, although Selma's obvious alcoholism caused some to speculate long before the councilman was found dead in the arms of something young, blond, and beautiful. And Selma knew that the abandonment of both her men—her husband and her son—were brought on by her own actions. Whether the councilman ever knew about Selma's tryst with her son's boyfriend, she could not tell. But soon after the incident, Councilman Fant could not stand to touch his wife, but was always savvy enough to never let his disgust show. Councilman Fant was the consummate politician. His game face was as unreadable as his heart, although it had not always been that way.

He must have known.

Shortly after the incident, after Earl-Anthony moved out, the marriage took on a cold ceremonial status. Intimacy was replaced by friendly indifference.

He knew. He must have.

Though they lived under the same roof, they had gone their separate ways, she to her videos, he to his Barbies. Selma's private media room was off-limits to the councilman and she never questioned his late-night meetings and overnights away from home.

And she missed him, missed him for all of the joy they once had before hell froze over. She missed him for that once-upon-a-time joy that he brought her; the laughs and the love and the child. And so she drank to him, to them both, ambivalently, all morning, noon, and night, almost each and every day.

Dee Bohannon was a cautious drinking buddy. She had spent all day Saturday after the funeral holding Selma's hand and drinking with her. And now here she was back on Sunday. She was not used to this. Her near-pristine liver had little time to dry out.

"Girl, I gotta drive down out these hills," she begged off with the hand when Selma tried to get her to have one more for the road. In one week of acquaintance they had become girl-friend enough for both of them to let their hair down to each other. Dee reminisced about the good husband she once had and Selma invited Dee into her private media room and shared her collection of homoerotica. The sight of men fucking men surprisingly turned Dee on. Watching men inside of men made her realize how much she missed Kevin inside her.

"You know when it really gets good?" Selma slurred, her eyes glued to the screen.

"When?"

"When they're doing each other and they don't think that anyone's watching."

"What?" Dee frowned incredulously.

"Oh now, don't get me wrong. This is all hot and wonderful and delicious, but when you're looking and they don't know you're looking, that's a tape worth cherishing."

"What in the hell are you rambling about, Selma?"

"Fantasies fulfilled," she answered with a strange, distant smile.

"I guess," Dee responded, not getting it; not sure if she wanted to.

It was getting late. The darkness of Selma's media room made Dee sensitive to the harsh sunshine pouring through the glass wall of Selma's foyer. She squinted furiously. Selma handed Dee a set of keys to her house as she walked her to the door.

"What's this?"

"Just in case. Anything might happen to me up in here, and Brando might not be around. He's got a set, too."

"Really?"

"And I've had a set of keys to his house since he moved in. When I first sold him the place. Good neighbor policy," she said with a strange slyness.

As Selma and Dee stepped out, Brando drove up into his driveway next door and beeped his horn. The two women waved at him and smiled as his garage door lifted.

"Since you're hangin' with the diva Fant, I hardly see you anymore," Brando called out to Dee playfully.

"Come on over for a drink," Selma flirted.

"Thanks, Selma. Got too much work."

"It's Sunday and it's beautiful." She pouted.

"Selma, I gotta go," Dee reminded her. "I'll call you later, Brando."

"See ya," he called back as he disappeared into his garage.

"That is one fine-ass piece of man," Selma drooled. "Too bad he's gay."

"Too bad for who?" Dee said as she got in her car and drove off with a wave.

Selma watched Dee's car disappear down the hill and thought to herself, with a strange doleful smile, Too bad for me.

Chapter Twenty-eight

Brando did some of his best work at home. He allotted this time to himself, before Senior Father Lacey Cannon's winter supper, to work, regroup, and chill out. This time alone with his thoughts was as much a part of his Sunday ritual as was his early-morning rise, the paper, the minimal workout, church, and brunch with Omar.

He studied the wording of the eighteen-page contract. The screen rights deal he'd negotiated for Clymenthia with New Line Cinema was straightforward and favorable to the novelist. But it had always been Brando's usual style to go over the simplest detail with a fine-tooth comb.

After three meticulous hours he signed off on the document and made a note to have his secretary overnight a copy to Clymenthia at the Mark Hopkins Hotel in San Francisco. He then rewarded himself with a refreshing skinny-dip in the pool. After several leisurely laps, he walked his dripping body over to the chaise and table, picked up his chilled glass of freshly pressed carrot juice, and rubbed it soothingly against his sparkling chest. He lowered the chaise to its flattened position and stretched out on his stomach. The feel of the sun on his wet torso, backside, and legs made him sigh like a beach bum. Church services earlier, brunch with Omar, and now this all made for the perfect Sabbath.

There are many black gay men who had not been abused as children, whether physically, sexually, or emotionally. And that sometimes somehow made them feel isolated in a world of the physically, sexually, and emotionally abused who spoke loudest.

There are many black gay men whose adolescent fears and anxieties were typical and developmental, in a world of fear and anxiety-induced atrophy.

There are many black gay men who are the grieving well, who suffer for those who suffer and give little time to suffering for themselves.

There are many black gay men who have attended "those meetings" of many of the black gay men's groups, only to find, more often than not, that so many of "those meetings" were vent sessions masquerading as support groups—the company misery sought, where unscarred men were looked upon with suspicion or, worse, pity for bearing little evidence of the everyday battle of living life as a black gay man.

Healing is the elixir sold by the charismatic snake doctors who write six-hundred-page books deifying pain, canonizing fear, and lecturing to the well and unwell, indiscriminately declaring all are sick, knowingly or unknowingly. And since all are sick, according to these self-fulfillers, all need healing. Those who profess wellness are either in deep denial or intellectually oblivious, naysayers say.

There are many black gay men who consider themselves

neither sick nor perfect. What they know is that they are God's perfect imperfect child, a good thing, whether their perfect imperfect brothers understand it or not. And perhaps that is why so many of these black gay men stay on the sidelines, passive and sublime, in the face of a community that sometimes prides itself on its ailments.

Brando was one of those many, knowingly or unknowingly, healthy black gay men on the sidelines. Suffering was not his m.o. His breakup with Collier was not painful. He loved Collier and he missed him, but not in a painful sort of way. Their relationship was complacent, too comfortable, even for him. Their parting of the ways was a good and gentlemanly thing, and he could not fathom pain in good and gentlemanly.

He did not suffer the pain of not being in love. Only the anxiety. Cautious anxiety. He accepted the fact that being in love was not a right. It was luck, a privilege, a gift, and the absence of being in love was not a curse; far from it. Love is special. Not plain wrap.

He appreciated the fact that he was a man perhaps backhandedly blessed merely by virtue of what he had in family and friends: physical health, heart, and temperament.

Still.

The painless void, the numbing lack of . . . *something.*

To, for once, not be impervious to the agony of the lovelorn heart. To, for once, cry over someone, cry for someone, cry for himself. To know what that would be like.

How he admired Omar, who cried at movies, during Oprah, at weddings, even when describing a memorable sexual encounter. Omar would cry when he got rid of a man or got dumped by a man. The drama of life was Omar's treasure. And this made Brando just a little jealous; jealous enough to recognize the feeling.

A feeling.

Chapter Twenty-nine

His solo performances were masturbatory works of art. Naked on the bed, his beautiful penis lay half alert and ready in its soft pubic nest. The way he stared at it, studied it way down there creeping and puttering up his stomach, past his navel, toward his nipple, was so innocent and clean and sexy. Watching the hand that found the propped-up knee and caressed it and worked itself gently down the thick calf and firm thigh was like watching a good dancer move to slow jazz. While the other hand, lathered with lube, stroked the bald-headed penis with a delicateness that made him whimper and purr.

How he carefully and caringly played with himself as the strokes took on a rhythm that picked up speed intensely.

Grabbing a handful of biceps, and then wetting a finger through soft shivering lips and caressing a nipple with moisture, he teased the slit of his tight-squeezing ass with that busy and slippery finger.

How he shook his head wildly and neighed and swallowed hard, and neighed and huffed as he shuttered and strangled his spastic and rock-hard eight inches.

How he shot all over her chest and his neck and his chin. How he lay there for what seemed like forever. But never long enough for her.

And then when Collier moved in it was almost too good to be true. Especially in the beginning, when their beautiful bodies were new to each other, ravenous and unquenchable; when they could not keep their hands off each other, could not keep their tongues and their fingers and their dicks out of each other; could not keep enough lube and clean towels in the cabinet.

How they grew beyond the hunger and learned to kiss with so much learned caring. How they learned to touch delicately because the delicateness of their perceived love must be adhered to.

And how they grew apart.

She saw it coming. Over the months she saw the signs even when they did not, way before they knew it. And there was no way to warn them.

Yet she stayed with them, prayed with them, mourned with them, and sadly chronicled the decline of their relationship. And if indeed the sex they started having near the end was an expression of their feelings for each other, then no wonder they parted company.

And yet . . .

That one special time when they made love knowing that it would be their last. That was a special time for them and for her. They cried in each other's arms. And Selma Fant cried as well when she viewed it on the discreetly installed and discreetly retrieved spycam.

Chapter Thirty

The new winter sun was typically bright and warm on this particular day in L.A. Senior Father Lacey Cannon's hillside terrace faced downtown, where the fantasy cluster of pastel buildings known as the Civic Center sparkled.

Brando always liked standing out here on Senior Father's terrace. It always seemed so peaceful here, this house so high up on Don Tomaso Drive. Even when filled with people, with party, it was eclectically peaceful with oxymoronic calm. Slow mellow jazz and a joviality special to vintage black homosexuals permeated the air.

Brando sipped his drink and listened to Kran Baxter and Delroy Meeks talk about the cruise along the Mexican Riviera they had just returned from.

The aroma of Senior Father's down-home cooking flowed through the house. Guests took turns peeking into the kitchen and licking their lips, engendering the wrath of their aproned host. Even out on the terrace Brando, Kran, and Delroy got a whiff, causing Kran to lose his place in his verbal home movies.

Omar and Shane arrived an hour after Brando, causing

133

Senior Father to beam with Big Mama glee. They acknowledged their host's hardy greeting with equal robustness and a bottle of good Napa Valley Chardonnay.

From the terrace, Brando saw them. He could tell that there was tension between Omar and Shane, again. He excused himself from Kran and Delroy and approached the new arrivals cheerfully.

" 'Bout time you guys got here," he teased, giving them both a big brotha man hug.

"Yeah, well, you know," Omar mumbled.

"He tried to talk me into not coming," Shane snapped, "but it didn't work."

Each year on November's third Sunday, Senior Father Lacey Cannon gave his winter supper. It was a warm and friendly affair, peopled by a core circle of black same-gender-loving men and their significant others, good girlfriends, new boyfriends, and loose trade; a well-heeled clique called the Older Set. Brando and Omar were but youngsters here. Shane was in swaddling cloth.

Every time the doorbell rang and the door opened a vintage high-pitched swell would soar gleefully above the soft jazz and cozy hum of conversation, announcing the arrival of yet another clubhouse member. Salt-and-pepper queens and other royals of great dignity held court here annually and lamented the passing of the golden post-penicillin, pre-AIDS days of skin-to-skin sex, cum swallowing, and back-to-back orgies. Gleeful reminiscences about Sylvester and Two Tons of Fun were lost on some of the DL youngsters too cool to know they were no more than house dressing.

"Man, this is really getting silly," Omar confessed to

Brando when he was able to get him alone. "This thing with Shane."

"So what's the problem now? Why didn't you want him to come?"

"Look around, Bran. Everybody's drinking. He's a fucking alcoholic."

"He seems to be handling himself all right."

"Yeah, for right now. But you don't have to deal with the shit later on, when like I get the blame for exposing him to all this."

Brando's cell phone vibrated in his pocket. He ignored it. Even checking the caller ID while his friend was bloodletting would be ill-timed.

"I'm sure you guys'll work it out. I mean, I'm sure he knows underneath that your intentions are caring."

"Yeah, right. He thinks my intentions are suspect."

"Are they?"

"Man, please. Come on, let's get a drink."

When Shane came out of the foyer guest washroom, he saw Omar and Brando out at the terrace bar, laughing and drinking like the old buddies they were and the new lovers they could easily be.

As far as Shane was concerned, this was just salt in the wound, especially considering what had happened the night before on Catalina Island.

"Well of course most gay men have money," Senior Father declared, holding court in his den, tipsy on after-dinner cocktails.

"How you think that?" Shane challenged, even as Omar tried to quiet him down. Senior Father smiled with a mixture of lust and condescension. Omar's beautiful young Puerto Rican was right up Senior Father's alley, though he would never think of trespassing.

"So many of us spend so much time isolated and ostracized, young man," Senior Father continued, a lecture for Shane, unneeded counsel for the cosigning, half-drunk guests in the room. "We are left to nothing but our own imaginations and our books and our plots and our drive to achieve in the face of monumental obstacles. And that drive, unencumbered by wives and girlfriends and unplanned parenthood, gives us an edge. And so we professionally focused men, who will hook up more often than not with other professionally focused men, create this great man gauntlet. And everybody knows that good, bad, or indifferent, the most powerful thing in this world is men united against everybody else. Of course most gay men have money. They're men squared."

"That is such a cliché," Shane tisked.

"It's a cliché because it's true, my beauty. Don't you agree, Brando?"

"I don't know, Senior Father," Brando answered. "It *is* a bit of a stereotype."

"Then you're a living stereotype, dear Bran," Senior Father declared triumphantly. "You're a successful entertainment lawyer, you drive a hundred-thousand-dollar Mercedes, you probably have a portfolio thick enough to choke a horse, your house is twice as big as mine—and I know what mine's worth, and I don't have a swimming pool. Now if I have money, which I do, thank you very much, I know you have money.

Look around this room. There's not an under-six-figure sissy household up in here."

"Hold up, G." Shane spoke up. "First of all, I ain't no sissy, and second, this room ain't representative of anything but a small segment of the black gay community, 'cause I ain't makin' no six figures."

"Sorry about the sissy part, my sweet, but if you combine your computer analysis and troubleshooting income with Omar's literary and journalistic booty, I'm sure you'd be well over six figures."

"Yeah, but who says me and Omar a couple?" Shane shot back.

A nervous pang shot through Omar so fiercely that he almost lost his high.

"No rings yet, but you're getting there." Senior Father was on a roll. "And when you and Collier were together," he continued, back on Brando, "what was he? A dentist? Not getting into your business, but I would have estimated your combined annual income at somewhere around half a mil? Close. You gay bros got buck. Lots of downpouring, disposable bucks, and no dependents to spend it on."

"Actually, ain't that kinda sad?" Shane asked facetiously.

"Now *that's* a cliché," Senior Father retorted, and there was an outburst of applause and cheers throughout the room. Omar stood up and let out with a drunken wolf yelp. Shane was embarrassed and pissed.

"You drink too damn much," he muttered to Omar under his breath, when Omar fell back down on the sofa next to him, laughing.

"And you don't fuckin' drink enough," Omar blurted

out, causing a pair of silver heads to look up and pause in synch.

The argument over whether Shane should have attended Senior Father's winter supper, or even this snippy social debacle, was not the source of Omar and Shane's latest quarrel. Tension had been brewing since they had made love on Catalina Island.

These are the facts.

Omar wanted to be bottom, which he did on occasion. But Shane obliged him so thoroughly that Omar called him out of his name. He called him Brando. Shane, however, was too deep in the get-good to stop, not insulted enough to pull out from the fabulous nut he was busting. Not insulted enough, that is, until the after-sex lull. He then grew quiet, and Omar could not figure out why.

"So what's up?" Omar broached the mood.

"What's my name, Negro?"

"Huh?"

"What's my damn name?"

"Shane. What's up, baby?"

"Next time you wanna be bottom, go get Brando to dick yo' ass down! *Pentejo!*"

Brando watched the Omar and Shane drama from the other side of the room, not aware that he was the wind causing the storm.

His cell phone vibrated again. Discreetly he pulled it out of his pocket and checked the caller ID. It was Jeanette Bell. He stepped out onto the terrace and answered the call.

"Brando," Jeanette answered with a strange calm.

"Hey, Jeanette, what's up?"

"I killed a man."

"What?" Suddenly everything was surreal. Brando looked back into the house where late-afternoon revelers were partying hardy while a friend was on the phone confessing the unthinkable.

"He raped me," she continued, suddenly allowing the strange calm to shatter under the weight of the scene brought back so vividly by her own words. "I killed him."

And then he heard the sobs.

"Baby—" He heard Clymenthia's soothing tone in the near distance. Then it was Clymenthia on the phone.

"It was self-defense, Brando."

"I'm sure the circumstances will support that," he stuttered, shaken but fighting it. "We need to get her someone to discuss this with, a lawyer."

"You're a lawyer, Brando."

"I'm an entertainment lawyer, Clymenthia."

"You're also a criminal lawyer."

"Used to be."

"You still are. We need you, Brando."

"When did this happen?"

"Last Sunday, after we left the restaurant. Near our hotel in Culver City."

"Has this been discussed with anyone else?"

"No."

"Good. Don't. I'm on my way."

Brando made his apologies to Senior Father. Omar, seeing Brando rush toward the door, caught up with him, leaving Shane in a funk back in the den.

"Bran, what's going on?" Omar could see the concern on his friend's face.

"Something's come up. I gotta go."

"Anything I can do?"

"Not right now, man, thanks."

"You sure?"

"Yeah, thanks."

The two friends hugged, and then Brando was out the door.

Chapter Thirty-one

The hour-long flight from Los Angeles to San Francisco could not have been smoother, but Brando's emotional turbulence brewed from anxiety and trepidation. Criminal law was a lot different from working out royalty points on a record deal, fine-tuning foreign book publishing rights, and jostling with the suits in the tinsel town towers. It had been a long time since he'd tackled criminal law. The dread of it all was reacquainting itself, reminding him why he had abandoned it for the pastel world of entertainment law.

But Jeanette was his friend and she needed him. He could only imagine the devastation she was experiencing after so heinous an attack. He only hoped he still had what it would take to serve her well.

His flight arrived in San Francisco at 10:39 PM. Forty-five minutes later a cab dropped him off at the Mark Hopkins Hotel on Knob Hill.

"I'm falling apart," Jeanette confessed to Brando after nearly an hour of tearfully retelling her terrible tale, "and you know me. I'm not used to falling apart. I'm not used to being like this."

"Would you like some more tea, baby?" Clymenthia asked her gently.

"Please," Jeanette answered.

"Bran?"

"No, thanks. I'm fine."

Clymenthia squeezed Jeanette's hand reassuringly, then got up and went into the service area of their hotel suite.

"I'm strong, a rock, resilient," Jeanette said to Brando, trying to convince herself. "But this thing? . . . I don't know . . ." She turned to Brando and looked him in the eye. "It's taken something out of me, Brando. I've been robbed of something I'll never get back."

"What you went through, Jeanette, nobody should have to go through. What you did to defend yourself was what you had to do. You're going to get through this."

"I will, Brando. I have to."

Throughout the night the three strategized. Brando convinced the two women that it was in Jeanette's best interest to return to the jurisdiction of the incident and to both file a complaint and surrender to what most assuredly would be charges ranging from third degree manslaughter to first degree murder.

"That's, more or less, a formality," Brando reassured them. "The burden is on the prosecution to disprove a self-defense claim instead of forcing a defendant to prove the action was justified. And the concealed weapon is a nonissue. You were duly registered and licensed as a rural resident of Connecticut with special circumstances related to previous harassment. The state of California is a cooperative to your home state's CCW statute."

Still, this was not going to be a cakewalk, and Brando knew

it. He stayed up all night and researched legal precedents on his laptop. The case of Patricia Carbone was chilling. In 1985 the Somerset County, Pennsylvania, woman was sent to prison for life on a first degree murder charge for killing the man she alleged abducted her and tried to rape her. Her defense? Self-defense.

The next morning Jeanette and Clymenthia flew back down to Los Angeles with Brando. Later that afternoon Brando entered the Culver City Police Department and filed rape charges on behalf of his client. He also informed the recording detective that his client had killed her assailant in self-defense. Detective Franklin looked up from an unrelated report she was filling out. She approached Brando.

"I'd like to talk to your client, Mr. Heywood."

"She'd like to talk to you, too, Detective. I'll have her here in an hour."

For the third time Jeanette Bell told the gruesome story, this time into an old police cassette recorder that whizzed coldly.

A court hearing was held the next day at 10 AM. By 10:15 Jeanette Bell was charged with a perfunctory second degree murder charge and released on her own recognizance. Awaiting Jeanette, Clymenthia, and Brando on the steps of the courthouse was a small group of reporters, tipped off that the lesbian partner of the Pulitzer Prize–winning novelist had been arraigned on murder charges stemming from the death of a Desert Storm war hero and alleged rapist. Brando shielded them as best he could and scurried them to his car. He had insisted that they stay at his home during the ordeal.

Dee heard about the case on the five o'clock news. She

called Brando. He was just getting Jeanette and Clymenthia
settled in when his cell phone rang.

"Unbelievable," Dee said when Brando answered the
phone. "How's she doing?"

"Pretty good, considering."

"Give her my best, Brando."

"I will."

"And if there's anything—"

"Thanks, Dee. Listen, I gotta go."

"I understand."

That night Brando, Jeanette, and Clymenthia sat in Brando's dark den before a crackling fireplace. Orange light illumi-
nated the furrowed brows, the searching eyes, and the brave
and comforting half smiles on their silent faces. They each held
and occasionally sipped at a glass of Merlot.

"You know something, Bran?" Jeanette finally said. "At
first . . . at first I was just going to let it pass. I killed the man
who did this to me . . . didn't I? He paid with his life . . . didn't
he? Just let it pass. Let it pass. That's what I was thinking. But
that's not what I was feeling. I couldn't. I couldn't let it pass.
Killing him? All I got was blood . . . now I want justice."

Chapter Thirty-two

Vanessa Ellerbee sat in the third pew of her husband's church and half listened to the sweet lies and slick garbage he spewed during the service. Her mind was filled with thoughts she knew were as wrong as his sermons, but she simply could not mask those feelings of growing desperation. William had spent the night out again, and the good sex she was usually rewarded with once he got home from fucking and getting fucked was diminishing. William had come home that morning a beaten man, unfulfilled, his thirst unquenched for what he fully needed, and so when he crawled in bed next to her, and then crawled inside her, he was only half there. He had not been spurred on. These mystery men of the night were now pulling him all the way over, and it was scaring her.

Oh, she believed that William was the genuine article, a bona fide bisexual who couldn't have one side and not the other. But this morning, when he came in, smelling of another man's soap and cologne, he only half made love to her, with that half of himself he doled out after giving too much to the male lover he had spent the night with. His lovemaking was mechanical, dutiful, distant, and distracted, as if suddenly it was a take-it-or-leave-it kind of thing, something that he could do without. He fucked her as if he expected her to fuck him back with dick she of course did not have. When he finished with her, it was the least fulfilled she had been after he had been with a man. Oh how she missed the fucking she got once her man was fucked down by the late DuPré Dixon.

She got up and showered and coiffed her church curls to perfection. The mirror was not her friend.

She looked into the face of a woman who was only half fulfilled, looked at her squarely, saw the face while she dressed in her Sunday finery, saw it as gospel music played on the radio while they drove to church, saw it as sisters in the congregation smiled at her, admired her, envied her, thought her so lucky to have such a fine man like handsome and caring Reverend William James Ellerbee.

When brothers greeted them, she thought she saw signal-filled, conspiring glances between William and them. She saw that face of hers thinking that it saw it, too.

She saw that damn face while William pitched purity and piety when she was so primed for pity. She saw it as she sat straight up during service, trying her best to maintain a preacher's wife's public decorum.

When the choir sang out, the face sang out, too, begging and pleading for her to join in. And when finally she did, her hands shot over her head and cut right through the air. Her tears flowed like streams, her moaning syncopated by hiccups in gospel rhythm. The nurse's attendants, armed with their smelling salts and restraints and their "There she goes again"s, took posts around her.

By the time the service was over, she was both sober and

sanctified, if not satisfied. She had a chance to rest from her sad happiness on the small cot in the sanctified lounge set up for these things. When she opened her eyes her husband was seated by her side.

"How are you?" he asked, squeezing her hand gently.

"I feel like some Lucy Florence," she answered, hoping and praying the new DuPré Dixon would be where he always was, with his friend at their usual table, having coffee and sweet potato pie, ready to help her keep her man home.

Chapter Thirty-three

Although Brando did not get into the details of the case, Omar listened attentively as Brando praised Jeanette's strength and Clymenthia's unwavering love and support. Brando's eyes sparkled with awe, his hands painting the air with the details of human persistence. He leaned in close toward Omar, who leaned in himself, and confessed how scared and driven he was.

"Brando?" came the voice that hovered over them.

"Hello—" Brando looked up, and then stood in the presence of her and the man that stood behind her. She extended her hand.

"Vanessa," she reminded him.

"Right. Vanessa."

"Vanessa Ellerbee."

"Yes, of course. Vanessa Ellerbee. Vanessa, I'd like you to meet Omar Stevens. Omar? Vanessa."

"Nice to meet you."

"Same here." Omar smiled as he stood.

"And this is William."

"Hello, William."

"Hi."

"Hi."

"Hello."

William was not as shy as he first seemed to be, nor as Vanessa had suggested. The way his eyes moved along Brando's lean body did not go unnoticed, and the overtness mildly annoyed and bemused all three in his company in very different ways. Vanessa resented the lack of subtlety and was now caught in a lie, harmless as it might have been, regarding William's alleged shyness. Brando's sense of propriety was put off by the extended and intrusive gesture, and Omar was quite simply jealous as hell. Yet all three pretended to ignore the elephant in the room and continued to exchange mock pleasantries.

"So what do you do, William?" Omar had successfully distracted William from his best friend's crotch.

"Pharmaceutical sales," William lied. "And you?"

"I'm a writer."

"Oh yes!" Vanessa chimed in. "Omar Stevens. I thought I recognized your name. I've read several of your pieces. I loved your piece on Keith Boykin's down-low book in the *LA Weekly*. It made me run right out and get it."

"Thanks."

"Of course I read J. L. King's book first, though it's not a problem I have to worry about." She gently squeezed William's hand.

"So," she continued, "where are you gentlemen off to from here? I'd love to invite you up to our place for cocktails."

"Thanks, Vanessa, but as it is, I'm already playing hooky from work I need to be doing."

"On Sunday?"

"Yep."

"All work and no play, Brando . . ."

150

"I know, I know." He chuckled good-naturedly. "But I really need to take a rain check."

"Too bad," William said with too much suggestion in his voice.

Vanessa tensed and forced a smile. She then eased into their good-byes, then presented her card. "You owe us a visit," she cautioned Brando with a slight peck on his cheek. "Doesn't he, William?"

"Absolutely," William answered, absently licking his lips.

"It's been a pleasure meeting you," she then said to Omar, suddenly remembering he was there.

Finding the slight too amusing to be offended, Omar watched the couple disappear down the stairs, walk past the open stage space, and out the glass door.

"Is it my imagination, but was sister girl trying to pimp her husband off on you?" Omar asked as he watched the couple walk toward the park and the Sunday drums.

"How do you know they're married?"

"You know, for a damn lawyer, you sure don't notice much. They had matching wedding rings, bro. You didn't see them?"

"I wasn't paying that much attention."

"Well he sure was payin' attention to *you*."

"Please."

"Now I know you noticed *that*. He was checkin' you out so hard you shoulda felt his tongue on your balls."

Brando shook his head and smiled, though his mind was on Jeanette.

Omar nudged. "So fill me in."

"On what?"

"The odd couple."

"There's really nothing to be filled in on, Omar. I met her at the Catch when I went to see Miss Zara. She said her friend, who was sitting across the room, wanted to meet me, but was kind of shy."

"Was nothin' shy about *that* dude."

"Yeah."

"So, you gonna go for it?" Omar pushed forward. "I mean, the brotha's not bad looking at all."

"I don't have time to be hooked up right now, Omar, especially with the case and everything."

"You can always take time for a hookup, bro."

Brando fluffed it off with a small flick of a hand.

Omar realized that maybe he was trying too hard. Pawning his friend and secret love off on this woman's fine husband was a masochistic exercise, giving away what he so needed to keep for himself.

All those years he secretly suffered but put up appearances and cheerleadered fiercely when Brando and Collier became the perfect poster board couple for L.A.'s black gay community.

And oh how happy and sad and gleefully mournful he was when their flawless reign ended.

If only Brando could love me the way I love him. Perish the thought. Not even. Act on it? Not even.

Omar regrettably realized he simply didn't trust the friendship enough to tell the truth.

Then what kind of friendship was it?

Maybe a friendship as bogus as the love affair he always imagined. He loved Brando, yet did not trust Brando enough to let him know.

Chapter Thirty-four

The district attorney for Los Angeles County knew that he faced an uphill battle—the strict precepts of law versus public empathy and perception. Who really was the victim in this case of *The People versus Jeanette Bell*? Although it could be argued that Ramon Jesse Alexander justifiably died at the hands of his alleged assault victim, it was not a clear case of self-defense. Besides, Alexander was a decorated war hero.

Vigilante justice is a front-heavy oxymoron in the eyes of the law. What seemed clear to the D.A. was that Jeanette Bell killed her alleged attacker *after* the alleged attack, not a legal defensive move. She had taken the law into her own hands and a man died. Her actions were vengeful at best, a vindictive response to scorn at worst; she was legally culpable. *The People versus Jeanette Bell* had all the markings of an open-and-shut case.

But this was L.A., a city that rarely convicted celebrities, even celebrities by association. The D.A. knew he had to put his best man on the job. And the best man for the job was a woman, Marion Madrano, a celebrity in her own right.

Marion Madrano was the Gloria Allred of the D.A.'s

office, passionate, publicity savvy, tough on crime, a champion of women victimized and abused. And that was of the utmost importance. No one else could better neutralize the built-in sympathy Jeanette Bell would most assuredly attract than the beautiful Latina legal star who worked herself up from the ghettos of Boyle Heights to the highest levels of City Hall, becoming one of the few conservative city officials in Mayor Villaraigosa's inner circle. What Gloria Allred, representing Amber Frey, had done for the late Laci Peterson and to Laci's murderous husband, Scott Peterson, Marion Madrano would have to do for this poor war hero, and to this woman of means and privilege who slaughtered him over possibly consensual sex. But at best, that was a crapshoot.

Marion Madrano met with Brando, Jeanette, and Clymenthia to offer a plea bargain of manslaughter. She did not need for this case to go to trial. She knew the liberal forces of the city would go into overdrive, that women, gays, and lesbians everywhere would unite through emails, chat rooms, rallies, talk shows, public demonstrations, Court TV, and Oprah in support of the defendant, a beautiful, Carnegie Mellon–educated femme fatale tailor-made for the camera.

Los Angeles was the land of the Simpsons: Bart, Jessica, Ashlee, and O.J. This was where the star of *In Cold Blood* stood trial and was acquitted of the cold-blooded murder of his wife of contrivance; where Michael's Neverland nursery trumped Disneyland. This was Kobeland, Magic's Kingdom, and Clintonville. The only crime in L.A. is to be lacking in entertainment value. A public trial for this kind of defendant was like a walk down the red carpet for a movie premiere at the Kodak Theatre.

But the plea bargain was flatly rejected and Marion Madrano was pissed. Uncharacteristically losing her cool, the frustrated officer of the court accused Brando's client of wanting to face charges in open court to publicize a cause.

"And you want her to cop a plea to silence her," Brando shot back with unusual force.

Prosecutor Madrano returned to her office and contemplated the cards she had been dealt. It was now a matter of figuring out which cards to play.

Chapter Thirty-five

All these people come here from other places—Detroit, Philly, Chicago, Brooklyn, whatever—and they all complain about what we do out here. And we L.A. people, the *real* L.A. people, we let them trip like that. They sit up here and never leave, just complain, laying up under our fuckin' palm trees, under our fuckin' year-round sunshine, in our mothafuckin' paradise. They all laugh at L.A. and can't wait to get here. Plastic. They call us plastic. Well at least we're *real* plastic . . . East Coast, arrogant-ass, bitter mothafuckas!"

Omar was drunk and ranting and feeling sorry for himself. Shane had finally given up on him and was moving back to New York after first calling Omar every fake-ass-airhead-shallow-old-young-wannabe-la-la-land pootbutt in the book.

Omar never really realized how much he cared for Shane. He never gave himself the chance to find out. And now with Shane gone, the very thought of not having him around left Omar pissy and pathetic.

Brando didn't say much. He had met with Omar this night to tell him that their Sunday-morning get-togethers at Lucy Florence would have to be curtailed, that their hanging out, clubbing, would have to be pulled back until after the trial. But suddenly hearing Omar's lament over this new development in his life put Brando in an emotional dilemma.

"Hell. Fuck it!" Omar declared. "Lovers come and go! Friends are forever!" He looked into Brando's sympathetic eyes and smiled a sad and drunken smile, then lifted his glass, urging Brando to lift his. "To friends," he continued.

"To friends," Brando repeated.

They clicked glasses gently. The ping hung in the air, illuminating the silence they now shared, a silence that hid feelings neither could verbalize. Under the dark amber lights, Brando saw a rarely seen yet oh-so-familiar look on Omar's face, that little-boy handsomeness that always appeared whenever Omar was sad and drunk, the look he saw whenever he and Omar were drinking and Omar drifted off into thoughts of his Grammy.

It was Tuesday night at the Study, that reliable watering hole just above Hollywood Boulevard on Western Avenue, where black gay men of all ages could always find a friendly shoulder to cry on and sympathetic bartenders heavy with the liquor and generous with a listening ear. Somebody had put on a half dozen Sade tunes. The droll from the box was relentlessly, poignantly forlorn.

"Did I tell you what happened to me last year at the hotel for ATB?"

At the Beach, L.A.'s annual black gay pride celebration, brought together some twenty thousand community members and their heterosexual allies from all over the world every Fourth of July weekend. The social convention featured well-organized seminars, networking events, banquets, barbeques, book signings, club hopping, and the centerpiece all-day beach party at Point Dume in Malibu. The host hotel was always sold out early, as much of the socializing took place there.

Omar always made sure he booked a room early. Better to be in snatching distance of the visiting honeys. And now he was in confession mode.

"Did I tell you what happened?" he repeated.

"No. But if it's too embarrassing maybe you shouldn't."

"Well it *is* embarrassing."

"Then maybe you shouldn't be telling me."

"Hey, I don't give a fuck. Shit happens and you just have to face it like a man."

"Okay, well then tell me."

"You know how all the young guys gather in the hotel lobby, right?"

"Yeah."

"Well at about three AM they expel them all from the lobby. So the kids all go up to the third floor and they just roam the hallways. So some old queen comes and bangs on my door and says, 'Chile, they roamin' the third floor.' And I know exactly what he means. So I get up, shower real quick, throw on something really nice—some Armani and shit, some khakis—and head down to the third floor. The kids, about five hundred of them, are barreling through the hallway like bulls on a Barcelona street. Hotel rooms are open, parties are going on, a little bit of everything is happening. So I join in and get swept up into the herd. Now as I'm being swept past this group of boys standing on the side, I hear this voice snickering: 'Look at that old queen out here trying to hunt up some young trade.'"

"Oh my God!" Brando laughed.

"Bran, I heard that, looked around, and realized I was the

oldest thing in the hallway. *I* was the old queen he was talking about."

"I am so sorry," Brando apologized.

"So I went back up to my room, never to be seen on the third floor again."

"Well that's what you get for being such a chicken hawk."

"Yeah, but what am I supposed to do? I can't help that I like what I like."

"Grow up, Omar. Grow up."

"That's a psychological impossibility."

"You are such a fool," Brando said, with just a touch of envy.

"But before I left the hallway, I saw who it was who said it."

"Who?"

"Some bitter boy I fucked once and never fucked again."

Brando marveled at the simplicity of the statement.

"That was his way of getting back at me. But I'll tell you one thing. Now that I've had that third-floor trauma, I can guarantee you, I'll never go through that again. That's why I gave up on Griffith Park."

"You gave up the park?"

"I gave up the park. I don't need a whole school of twenty-five-and-unders reminding me how old I am and how old I'm getting."

"So are you saying you're giving up on the young?"

"Well, I can't totally deny my nature, but I'll just not lurk around their nurseries, their natural habitats. That's much too tempting."

Brando found himself smiling as he remembered the days when he and Omar were twenty-five-and-unders, out of school for the summer and living the lives of two Southern California black surfer boys, gleefully trolling the Venice Beach boardwalk, gawking at impossibly chiseled bodybuilders flexing muscles and shirtless, golden, sweaty basketball players selling wolf tickets and executing court steps Twyla Tharp would love to steal. Splashing in the Pacific and riding the waves just north of the Santa Monica Pier was Omar and Brando's daily duty; clubbing till daybreak in every afterhour venue still jumping, from the Rage in West Hollywood to the Executive Suite in Long Beach; passing out next to each other in the house Omar's Grammy left him, waking up wondering why limbs were twined; morning hard-ons peeked through boxer slits, spooned like old-time lovers, and not wondering. In those days they weren't that concerned with boyfriends and romance. They had each other, and that was good enough for them.

Omar had already started writing articles on artists like Prince, Michael Jackson, DeBarge, Vanity 6, and Kool & the Gang for teen fan mags *Right On!*, *Black Beat*, and *Seventeen*. The publicity department of every major record label kept him supplied with concert tickets to every act that performed in the city. Omar and Brando were press regulars at the Greek Theater, the Hollywood Bowl, the Santa Monica Civic Auditorium, the Long Beach Arena, and the Roxy on the Sunset Strip.

Life was good to them, and if they were not such perfect brothers, they would have made perfect lovers.

"Remember when we were young?" Brando asked Omar, finding sparkles in his eyes.

"I remember." Omar smiled. "Going to the clubs, dancing our asses off while over in the corner holdin' up the wall was the grandfathas, leering and sipping their Hennessy. And I remember saying, 'When I get that age, don't let me end up like that. Just put a damn bullet in my head.' "

"There's a lot to be said for getting older," Brando said softly, "and besides, there are a lot of kids who like the maturity of older guys."

"Geezer chasers," Omar snapped heartily.

"I don't know about all that, but there are some young guys that simply like the maturity."

"And experience. It takes experience to really know how to fuck."

"Why does everything have to be about sex with you, Omar? That's all you talk about."

"Hell, Bran, if more people in the black community talked about sex more we wouldn't have all these damn problems. Denial's gonna be the death of us."

"Yeah, but you seem to be obsessed with sex."

"I'm obsessed with life, baby. *Life!*"

"All I know is it takes experience to know how to love," Brando said out of nowhere.

"Oh Miss Oprah, please. What the fuck would you know about love?"

Brando knew that what Omar said was not meant to hurt. It was merely a truth rarely spoken out loud.

"You are such a queen," Brando retorted.

"Everybody's a queen, Miss Brando. Queening is a natural thing. Will Smith queens. Wesley Snipes queens. Bill Clinton queens. To queen is just to address a bad situation with a little style, wit, and grace."

Chapter Thirty-six

Peter Caise had not been back to Los Angeles in years. His Southern California screwups were compounded by his escape to Detroit on a piece of good ass disguised as true love. His relationship with Eddie Jessup in Detroit turned out to be a total lose-lose situation. He figured it was bad karma well deserved. His own trifling ways over the years could not have produced anything more than the bullshit his life had been filled with since leaving Los Angeles.

He actually believed that Eddie loved him, or tried to believe it, but deep down inside Peter knew that Eddie didn't love anybody but himself. Eddie didn't love his wife, and Eddie didn't love his children. How could he and still have a man fucking him on the side?

Peter Caise first met Eddie Jessup at a downtown gym in L.A., a block and a half from the Staples Center, when the Detroit Pistons were playing the Lakers in the finals. Eddie was an off-the-radar Piston second stringer on the serious DL who had convinced Peter to follow him to Detroit, where Eddie set him up in a swank Jefferson Boulevard apartment overlooking the Detroit River.

Peter knew allowing himself to be a kept man was his first mistake. The second was to confuse great fucking with great lovemaking. Eddie was truly a great fuck who was equipped with a tight, lean, probasketball build that boasted rock-hard pecs, a thick dick, and a hungry, high-hoisted ass Peter had to climb to get to. Like a lot of these beautiful but macho, semi-celebrity, body-by-Fisher-brains-by-Mattel undercover brothers, Eddie Jessup wanted that occasional reprieve from marital and image duty that called for him to do all the fucking, be the pollinator, never the flower. On occasion, Eddie Jessup wanted to sit on something big, stiff, warm, and ass-filling. His sugar walls had needs, too.

He had heard stories of white boys who got their wives to strap on dildos and lay the pipe fantastic, but ask that of a black woman? Eddie knew better than to even go there. Besides, toys weren't his thing. He needed the natural feel of a man's true nature up inside him.

Peter knew Eddie was lying when Eddie told him he was the first man he ever let fuck him. A loose ass speaks volumes. Peter wondered often why so many women never thought to examine more closely those grand husbandly canyons.

A couple of years after Peter walked out of Eddie's life, he read that Eddie's wife, Aisha, had contracted HIV. Once it was discovered that Eddie was also infected, accusations flew back and forth. But deep down inside Eddie knew. Aisha Jessup had not been with another man in the seven years she had been married to Eddie. Eddie, however, had been with dozens, though he finally fessed up to her and the press that he obviously contracted the virus from any of the numerous female groupies he indulged on the road—lie that it was—women he swore on his mother's grave he would never go near again. This, ironically, was one of his few spoken truths.

Right from the start, when Peter and Eddie first got together in Los Angeles, Peter put his foot down and his glove on.

Peter Caise certainly had his ways, but he never considered himself stupid. Eddie was into barebacking, skin-to-skin, as if the AIDS epidemic never happened. But Peter wasn't about to put his life at risk over a piece of ass, no matter how much he thought he might love the man wearing it. And he thought he loved the man a lot.

While being kept, he did not simply sit in that riverfront apartment wringing his hands and watching soaps like some dick-dangling hausfrau at the beck and call of an NBA second stringer. He allowed his art to flourish.

And when he finally left Eddie, he utilized his arts degree and talent and found work as a graphic artist and website designer.

He also found himself. He had hated himself for so long, hated himself for not having a conscience. But in those final months as a disingenuous concubine to a ballplayer who sweated, grunted, and whimpered beneath his disinterested pumping, he would think about Aisha Jessup and wonder what lie had been told to get at this tryst. That's when he realized he had been doing this kind of shit since screwing Earl-Anthony Fant's mother.

So during the day, back in Detroit, when he did not want to think about Aisha Jessup, did not want to think about Earl-Anthony Fant and Earl-Anthony's mother, did not want to think about what he had become, he would draw, sketch, and write. The small graphic novel he produced from these escapes was as dark and as poignant as a tale out of Grimm.

And now he was back in L.A., where everything seemed to move in slow motion, which was just fine with him. He needed to slow down, assess his situation, figure it all out, figure himself out. He had been told that he didn't like himself very much, years ago, by Earl-Anthony. And he knew that the words did not come out of pain that he inflicted, but they were words of sad assessment . . . and truth.

He welcomed a confrontation with that truth and himself. He soon learned to stop loathing himself for loving men. He had fully come to realize that heterosexuality was just not in his nature, no matter how fiercely he fought for it, no matter how strongly fundamentalists preached fire and brimstone against what every feeling of love and desire cried out from *his* heart, *his* soul, *his* body.

Being back in Los Angeles was a good and necessary thing. It was an obligatory return to the scene of the crime, a step closer toward purging. It was a step closer toward seeing Earl-Anthony again, to seek forgiveness. And it was a chance to meet Miss Zara for the very first time.

Chapter Thirty-seven

Because of the upcoming trial, Brando was not able to spend as much time as he would have liked with Omar, and he missed his friend, more than he realized. They missed each other. Even their Sunday brunches at Lucy Florence had to be put on hold. But both understood, or at least tried to.

Dee checked in often with Brando and kept Selma Fant posted on the proceedings, although the papers and local news kept tabs on what was poised to be another Hollywood courtroom drama. Even the NAACP got into the picture. Cosigned by the ACLU, it made careful comments about the media digging up graves to find black men to demonize, without ever once mentioning the Bell case specifically.

Judge Canton W. Stork presided over the trial that convened less than six months after Jeanette Bell's indictment on second degree murder charges.

In her opening statement, prosecuting attorney Marion Madrano quickly established the given rapport between her and the six men and six women who were as black, white, brown, and yellow as the city itself. She spoke warmly to them like sisters and brothers, like family members that she would lay down her life for.

"You are the people of the County of Los Angeles," she reminded them gently, "and I represent you, I am one of you. I want you all to understand that a great crime committed against one of us is a great crime committed against all of us. Ramon Jesse Alexander was a decorated war hero who risked his life not only for his brothers and sisters on the battlefield but for the freedom of all of us, his brothers and sisters here at home. I will prove to you that a great crime was committed against Lieutenant Alexander. I will prove that a woman, carrying a concealed weapon, killed this unarmed war hero. Now the defendant will no doubt claim self-defense. Who knows? We'll see. One thing we do know is that it's her word against his. Oh, that's right. She killed him. He's not here to speak for himself. And because of that, you and I—we *must* speak *for* him."

She stood in front of the jury box and looked into the eyes of each and every one of them. She smiled a small smile of sad sympathy and reverential remembrance. She made them remember their lost brother, the pact that they must make, the duty that was theirs from this moment on until final deliberation.

Quietly, she walked back to the prosecution table.

Brando, holding Jeanette's hand, was slow to rise from his chair. He approached the twelve solemnly.

"When soldiers go to war," he began, "we understand they might kill. They might kill to save others, they might kill to save themselves. They certainly might kill to preserve our freedoms. Killing is a defense of last resort. I think we all understand that. I think that is the reason the founding fathers gave us the right to bear arms, so that, if it comes to that, we will have the right to protect ourselves from harm, even if it means killing. Many women in this country are kidnapped, raped, brutalized, and murdered. Perhaps that is why so many states in our United States allow certain people under certain circumstances to carry concealed weapons. Miss Bell is one of those legally granted that allowance. And thank God for it. It just may have saved her life. Killing is not pretty, but sometimes it becomes a necessary resort. When a man, even a soldier, becomes a monster, each and every one of us has a right to protect ourselves from his monstrosity. We have the right, if necessary, to protect ourselves to the very death."

The prosecution's first witness, Detective Edetta Franklin, answered all of Madrano's questions with total professionalism. The detective understood that Jeanette Bell put a face on a rape too many victims were too afraid or ashamed to.

But she could not think about the regret that threatened to boil up inside her. She was a professional, a law enforcement officer, an instrument of the law. She had to think of duty, although she herself was a woman who had been wronged enough to regret by the grace and vengeance of God that she did not do to her attacker what Jeanette Bell had done to hers.

"Is it true, Detective, that the defendant waited a week before confessing the killing to the police department?" Madrano questioned.

"Yes."

"And is it also true that the defendant showed little remorse in recounting what happened?"

"Objection!" Brando protested. "That calls for an expert medical opinion."

"Detective Franklin is a well-trained officer of the Culver City Police Department," the prosecutor countered, "well trained to psychologically profile the accused."

"The detective has a badge, Your Honor," Brando countered, "not a medical degree."

Judge Stork sustained the objection and the prosecutor ended her questioning. Brando felt no need to cross-examine the detective. Her neutral testimony gave neither side points.

The coroner was called next. His testimony corroborated many of the D.A.'s contentions, particularly that the deceased was shot twice in the back, which suggested a possible retreat, not an attack.

"How many times was the deceased shot totally?" Brando asked on cross-examination.

"Six times," the coroner answered.

"And where was he shot?" Brando then asked, retrieving a copy of the autopsy report from the defense table.

"Twice in the buttocks, once in the head, once in the shoulder, and twice in the groin area."

"And where was he shot first?"

"Trauma would suggest in the buttocks."

"Would suggest?"

"Yes."

"Meaning the deceased being shot in the buttocks first is not an absolute certainty."

"That is correct."

"So is it possible that he could have been shot first in the shoulder, spun around by the impact, then shot in the buttocks, continuing in a spin, then shot in the head and groin area?"

"Possible but highly unlikely."

"Is it *possible*, Doctor, yes or no?" Brando insisted.

"Yes," the coroner surrendered.

The next day, Marian Madrano called Tyler Martin to the stand, and he testified for the prosecution just as he had been coached to. His life had been saved on the front lines of Kuwait during Desert Storm. He was living proof of Ramon Jesse Alexander's heroism.

Brando knew he had a tough road ahead of him and did not take for granted the great confidence Jeanette and Clymenthia had in him.

He saw many faces in the courtroom. Clymenthia Teager was, of course, there every day; sometimes Dee; but once he even thought he saw Collier, and it gave him an unexpected heaving.

Yet he still did not ever lose sight of the gravity of the case and his need to focus solely on securing the exoneration of a woman and a friend who faced fifteen years to life if found guilty, a human being treated inhumanly and who responded emotionally, passionately, without a moment of premeditation; feelings he once experienced and had somehow lost touch with. Why had he allowed Earl-Anthony's rebuff to armor him against love so deeply? Why had he spent ten years with Collier and not one day matching the love he received? Why had he forgotten the sorrow he felt when Omar cried in his arms? Why had he not remembered the beauty of that one night that they made love? Why had he treated himself so inhumanely?

Suddenly realizing the deep pain of inhumane treatment, he knew. He knew what he had to do for Jeanette. It was all coming back to him. Yes. The jury was just a dozen ordinary people looking to do the right thing by listening, and attempting to be fair in the face of human imperfection, his imperfection, Jeanette's, theirs, even the seemingly perfect witness for the prosecution sitting on the stand giving glowing testimony about Jeanette's attacker. The jury was looking to be fired toward the truth—that no one deserves to be treated as if they're less than human. No one should ever do that to another person. No one should ever do it to oneself.

But the embers had to more than smolder. They had to flame into a light that would make the jurors see.

Brando Heywood understood more fully at this very moment, as Tyler Martin spoke so well of Ramon Jesse Alexander, that there were darker forces to be unveiled, and new light waiting to shine through.

"Was Ramon Alexander a good soldier?" was Brando Heywood's first question to Tyler Martin.

"Yes he was," Tyler answered.

"How many men did he kill when he saved your life?"

"Three."

"How many men would you say he killed altogether?"

Tyler hesitated, then answered, "Twenty-seven."

"How would you know that?"

"He told me."

"So he kept track of his kills."

"A lot of soldiers did."

"So he *did* keep track of his kills."

"Yes."

"Did he seem proud of his kills?"

"He was proud of doing his job."

"Did he seem proud of his kills, yes or no?"

"Yes."

"How many women did he kill?"

"Sometimes civilians got caught in the crossfire."

"How many women did Ramon Alexander kill?"

"I don't know."

"None? Some?"

"Some."

"Do you know a Captain Michael Simmons?"

"Yes, he was our platoon leader."

"Do you recall Captain Simmons saying to Ramon, 'Watch your mouth, Alexander'?"

"Yes."

"Was this right after Ramon killed a woman?"

"Yes."

"Do you remember what Ramon said to prompt Captain Simmon's verbal reprimand?"

"Yes."

"What did Ramon say?"

Tyler looked around the room, then lowered his head. "He said . . . 'Got me another one of them fuckin' Arab bitches.'"

Chapter Thirty-eight

Omar sat alone at his and Brando's table at Lucy Florence and sipped absently at his mimosa. One of the twins brought him a slice of sweet potato pie.

"You look like you could use this," the twin said.

"Thanks," Omar responded, looking up with a small smile.

As the twin walked away, Omar saw the woman. Vanessa. Vanessa Ellerbee. That's her name. And she was alone as well.

She noticed him staring at her and became perplexed by the empty chair next to him.

They nodded at each other cordially. Vanessa then stood and walked toward Omar's table. Church curls bounced in slow motion. Omar stood.

"Vanessa."

"Omar."

"Solo this week?"

"Seems we both are."

"Sit. Join me."

"Are you sure?"

"Of course. Please."

He guided her into the chair usually reserved for Brando and Brando alone, gently tucking her under the linen ledge of the table. He then sat and scooted in closer.

Yes, she thought, getting another good close-up look at Brando's second. *He is much too self-centered, too sinfully gorgeous, too much of a cad for fucking my man and giving him back; too unpredictable, too wild for the job. Oh no. Uh-uh-uh. If all else fails with Brando, this one could not even be a consideration.*

"What were you thinking?"

"Excuse me?"

"You had this look on your face."

"Really?"

Omar stopped one of the twins and ordered two more mimosas. Neither knew where to begin so they filled in the awkwardness by discussing the weather.

On their fourth round of champagne and orange juice they got around to Brando. Vanessa was straightforward about her intentions. She needed a man to keep hold of her man, and Brando was the one.

Omar listened coolly, not knowing whether to be put off or turned on by her candor. Then resentment started to brew, ever so slightly. Her condescension, her faux fag-haggishness, her sympathy-seeking confiding as if he was her sissy-mammy hairdresser was beginning to piss him off.

"My husband is bisexual," she continued. "I accept that. I have no choice. I love him. He loves me. But he has needs I can't fulfill. Now I don't want him out there with every Tom, Dick, and Harry. I need someone safe, dependable, someone to fulfill that other side of him, not someone to fall in love with him. I think Brando would be perfect for him."

"And what makes you think that Brando is that kind of freak?" Omar finally asked.

"What makes you think that he isn't?" she asked back. "William finds him very attractive. I find him very attractive for William. And I am all about pleasing my husband, by any means necessary."

"So what's *your* story?" Omar then asked. "You like to sit back and watch?"

"I sit back, I watch, I wait my turn."

"Our Lady of the Leftovers," he said, thinking out loud.

"Excuse me?"

"I don't know you that well, Vanessa, but let me tell you something—"

"What can you possibly tell me?" she asked incredulously.

"I can tell you this. You're a fucking idiot."

"Excuse me?"

"You are," he went on, knowing the booze was doing most of the talking. "Why the hell would you want to be with a man you can only half fulfill, who can only half fulfill you? What is wrong with you? Your husband may be straight, which I doubt, but his dick is gay, his asshole is gay. He wants what you want. What else do you need to know? Think better of yourself, lady. Think better of your womanhood, for God's sake. Get you a man who needs all of you, because there's a part of your husband that you can't satisfy. Realize it, get over it, stop shoppin' for him, and move the fuck on away from my man."

"*Your* man?" she asked derisively, eyes rolling. Now she was pissed off.

"Yes," Omar snapped, rolling his eyes right back, "my man. Brando."

"Brando?" She then laughed, hooted actually, in spite of the read-down. "Shiiit," she said in a ghetto-fabulous voice she had spent a lifetime repressing, "you just as fuckin' deluded as me."

Brando was too preoccupied with the trial for his ears to be burning, but he had talked to Omar earlier that morning.

Omar's breakup with Shane had slowed him down considerably, had decidedly changed the tone of his voice. Brando noticed that. There was something different about the way Omar sounded—a new softness in his voice, introspection, a maturity melancholied by some strange longing that was not just the residue slathered from losing Shane.

Omar had broken up with lovers before and the melodrama was usually over the top and gotten over quickly. But this was different. Omar was different, and Brando wasn't quite sure why.

Brando made a mental note to save next Sunday for Omar. Their friendship deserved it. Their brotherhood deserved it. Their love for each other deserved it.

Chapter Thirty-nine

Engagements in New Orleans, Atlanta, D.C., Philadelphia, San Juan, Saint Louis, and Chicago filled Miss Zara's schedule, and in each city she packed the clubs with her diva faithful. Omar had been commissioned by *Clik* magazine to do a profile on her.

She was now back in Los Angeles and ready to sit down for the interview. Omar was the perfect choice. He was a friend. He knew her well enough to tell her story honestly, boldly, with a decided sense of humor and a bit of fudge, with just enough bittersweet sadness.

While so many others did not, could not get what she was all about, Omar understood her, from one motherless child to another.

"I am so sorry I missed your show, doll," he said when they hugged and kissed upon his arrival at her Rossmore Avenue penthouse. The resplendent Art Deco apartment had been home to silver screen vamp Mae West during the last forty years of the platinum blond's life.

"Yeah, I heard you had trade at the last minute." Miss Zara smirked.

"Well, I ain't the one no more, now that I turned in my ho' card." Omar chuckled, allowing himself to be led by the satin-clad diva into the study where spotless, floor-to-ceiling French doors opened out to the Los Angeles Country Club golf course below.

"Heard that, too," Miss Zara said as she settled elegantly into the softness of a brocade-and-silk-covered chaise that sat in front of an eighteenth-century étagère that displayed various awards well earned throughout her career.

Omar sat in the leather high-back across from her. Eli entered and placed a sterling tea set on the table before them. Miss Zara would not let her man leave without first getting a small kiss and a deep whiff of his musk-scented body wash. As he walked out of the room she marveled at the familiar thick legs and calves and firm bubble butt moving unconsciously sensual under snug-fitting jeans.

"How's Brando?" she then asked. "How's he coming with the case?"

"It's got him going," Omar answered with a sigh as he set up his tape recorder. "Actually, I haven't seen much of him lately. We talk on the phone now and then, but I haven't really seen him."

"And you miss him."

"Well, yeah. I'm used to having him around."

"You're in love with him, aren't you?"

"Hey, look, we're here to talk about you, okay?"

"Okay." She smiled.

Chapter Forty

"If I had been there, I would have killed him," Clymenthia Teager testified on cross-examination from Madrano. It was the first day of the defense's case. Brando had gotten the jury's sympathy with Clymenthia's testimony. But now the prosecution was asking the questions.

"Jeanette Bell is my family," Clymenthia continued. "To protect her I would have killed her attacker. I would have done what anyone whose family member was being attacked would have done."

"You would have murdered him for what he did?" Madrano questioned carefully.

"Yes," Clymenthia answered without a blink.

"And do you think it was okay for Jeanette Bell to murder Mr. Alexander?"

"Objection, Your Honor," Brando called out. "The use of the term 'murder' with regard to my client is prejudicial. Murder is an unlawful killing, and until this jury determines that Miss Bell's actions were unlawful, Miss Madrano should not play hard and fast with so serious and inflammatory a term."

"Sustained," Judge Stork ruled.

"Then let me put it this way," Madrano said. "Do you think it was okay for Jeanette Bell to *kill* Mr. Alexander?"

"Under the circumstances, yes."

Marion Madrano was a great respecter of the dramatic pause. She allowed the witness's answer to hang in the hush of the courtroom, an echo, a seeking of revenge, a cry for blood. She then looked over at the jury, twelve ordinary citizens listening to a rich and famous lesbian defending her girl who'd killed a man.

"No more questions for this witness."

As Marion Madrano returned to the prosecution table, Brando, too, considered the jury. In spite of inherent sexual-orientation and socioeconomic prejudices that worked against his client, he was convinced that one woman's support of another woman's defense against rape still had a persuasive chance. He called Dr. Eleanor Jamison to the stand.

Dr. Jamison gave detailed descriptions of Jeanette Bell's injuries. The blown-up photos of her bruised body dramatically underscored the violence of the act. The doctor's dispassion in recounting her examination lent great credence to her statements.

"In my opinion, Jeanette Bell was raped," she concluded.

"Thank you, Dr. Jamison," Brando responded softly. He then turned to Prosecutor Madrano. "Your witness."

"Dr. Jamison," Madrano began as she rose from her seat, "what did Jeanette Bell say happened to her that night to cause the injuries in question?"

"She said it was a wild night that got out of hand."

"A wild night with a man, correct?"

"Yes."

"No further questions."

As Madrano moved back toward the prosecution table, Brando rose quickly. "Redirect, Your Honor."

"Proceed, Counselor."

Brando approached the witness. "Dr. Jamison," he began, "when Miss Bell said that her injuries were due to a wild night with a man, did you believe her?"

"No."

"In your professional opinion, what did you believe?"

"Objection, Your Honor," Madrano interrupted. "Asked and answered."

"Sustained."

"Dr. Jamison, did you encourage your patient to report this incident to the police?"

"Yes."

"Did you encourage her to report the incident because in your professional opinion you believed she was a victim of a crime?"

"Yes."

"Is it uncommon for rape victims *not* to report this kind of crime?"

"It's not uncommon at all."

"Why is that?"

"Many reasons. Shame, fear of retribution, the victim being made out to be the villain."

"You mean like what is happening today in this court?"

"Objection!" Madrano screamed heatedly.

"Mr. Heywood," Judge Stork threatened.

"No further questions, Your Honor."

Charlene Alexander then took the stand. Under Brando's careful probing, she described years of abuse she suffered at the hand of her husband—sexual torture, beatings, threats against her life. With great caution Brando road-mapped the alleged rapist's history of violence.

"Was he like that in the beginning?" he asked solemnly.

"No," his widow answered.

"When did you notice the change?"

"When he got back from the Middle East."

"What was different about him, in your opinion?"

"He treated me like the enemy. He enjoyed hurting me."

"Objection!" Madrano jumped up. "This goes to the witness's unqualified assessment of the victim's state of mind."

"Your Honor, this is his wife," Brando protested, "a woman who suffered years of spousal abuse—"

"And who did not file one police report," Madrano interjected loudly.

"Because she was afraid to!" Brando bellowed.

Judge Stork considered both litigators with careful eyes. "Overruled," he said finally.

Brando continued to question the witness. "How much do you weigh, Mrs. Alexander?"

"A hundred and thirteen pounds."

"And how much did Ramon weigh?"

"Two hundred and sixty pounds."

"Thank you," Brando then said softly. As he headed toward the defense table, Madrano rose immediately to her feet and began her questioning without hesitation. She did not want the image Brando had painted to linger any longer in the jury's mind.

"Mrs. Alexander, let me first say how truly sorry I am for your loss of your husband. I understand. I'm a widow myself." Technically, Marion Madrano *was* a widow. The first of her three husbands had died weeks before their divorce was finalized.

"Thank you," Charlene Alexander responded.

"Was your husband a good provider, Mrs. Alexander?"

"Yes."

"Did you love him?"

Charlene Alexander thought about how things used to be between her and Ramon, in the beginning. He was a gentle bear of a man when they first started dating, the man she married, the man that went off to war. But he was not the same man when he returned. She missed the man she first knew. She had mourned his loss from the day he got back from Kuwait.

"Yes," she finally answered, tears welling in her eyes, "I loved him."

"Thank you, Mrs. Alexander. No more questions."

Chapter Forty-one

Court adjourned for the weekend. It was two o'clock. Saturday morning. Brando sat alone in his living room, pondering many things, every angle, searching his mind for stones unturned, torturing himself for the inadequacies he believed plagued his defense. Marion Madrano was a formidable opponent whose skills and, indeed, activism for the rights of women he greatly admired. She would be the last person to go after a rape victim, unless she believed that the rape victim was not a victim at all. That, he knew, was how the jury could see it, see this delicate daughter of migrant workers fighting for the rights of a dead war hero, gone too soon.

"You're doing just fine," Clymenthia said to him softly, startling him out of his conflicted train of thought. "Truth will trump perception, Brando."

"What are you doing still up?"

"Same as you. Thinking about the case."

"Where's Jeanette?"

"Out like a light. That's how much confidence she has in you."

"What about you?"

"I agree with her. Now all we need is for you to agree."

With a small smile he conceded.

"Thanks," he said.

She hugged him.

"I need this, too," he said, still in her embrace.

"You also need to go be with your boy Omar."

"I know. We're getting together for brunch tomorrow."

"Good. It'll take your mind off the trial for a second; let you clear your head."

"Clym?"

"Yeah?"

"Collier was in the courtroom the other day."

"I know. I saw him. He's very proud of you."

"Did he say that?"

"Yes."

"So you two spoke?"

"Yes."

"What else did he say?"

"He wished he could have stuck around to tell you personally."

"You think it's true what they say?"

"About what?"

"You can't go back?"

"Oh, I don't know. All I know is I'm not a big fan of 'can't.' Do you still love him?"

"I'm not sure. It's just that I've been thinking about him a lot lately. You know, I've always been a little envious of you and Jeanette."

"Why?"

"I don't think I've ever had what you two have."

"It's haveable, baby. It really is. But it doesn't just happen. Now get some sleep. Dream about Collier. Then do something about it."

"Thanks."

Chapter Forty-two

That Sunday found Omar and Brando arriving separately at
their favorite table at Lucy Florence. The renewal of the
ritual made Omar feel awkward, but the warmth of their meeting eyes, enthusiastic smiles, and tight hug confirmed that their
friendship had not lost a beat.

Neither Brando nor Omar noticed Vanessa and William
Ellerbee staring at them from across the crowded room.

The two handsome men sat down at the table with great
gusto, then leaned across it with cool conspiratorial snickers.
They were like kids at a private school plotting harmless mis-
chief. They updated each other on things they already knew.
Omar had been following the trial through the media, and
Brando praised Omar on his recently published profile of Clymenthia Teager in *Essence*. Given the present situation, the article took on a new poignancy.

"Clymenthia loved it," Brando said.

"I know," Omar said, barely able to keep his eyes from
staring longingly. "She sent a nice thank-you note."

"So what's been happening, man? How's the track runner
and the Silver Lake thug prince?"

"Who knows?" Omar sighed. "I kinda kicked them to the curb. Or maybe they kicked me to the curb. There hasn't been anybody since Shane."

"Really?"

"Really. But I'm over him. We had some good times together. I even forgave him for reading me the riot act."

"You sort of deserved it, Omar."

"Yeah, I guess I did, huh?"

"Yeah, I guess you did."

"So now I'm a new member of *your* club."

"And what club is that?"

"Celibacy Anonymous."

"Please." Brando half laughed.

"It's true," Omar defended good-naturedly. "I haven't had sex in like six weeks."

"That's not celibacy, Omar, that's a breather."

"For me that's celibacy. The last time I went without sex that long was when I covered the Sparks exhibition tour through the former Soviet bloc back in ninety-nine."

Brando had to laugh. Omar was still the same old Omar. Had it only been a month since they last saw each other? It seemed so much longer.

"There's your girl," Omar said, looking up.

"Excuse me?"

"And your boy."

Omar nodded and waved at someone behind Brando's back. Brando looked over his shoulder. Vanessa Ellerbee was nodding back at Omar; then, catching Brando's eye, she smiled invitingly. William perked up. Brando gave them both a cordial thumbs-up and returned his gaze back to his friend.

"Are you going to call them?" Omar asked, after casually sipping his coffee.

"I don't think so. I'm not that kind of freak."

"Yeah. Right."

"Omar, how long have you known me?"

"Too long. Not long enough."

"Being hooked up with a man by his wife is a little too deep for me. You know that's not me."

"Do I?"

"Besides, I'm looking for love, not just sex."

"God, you're so pure I can't stand it."

"Well, one thing I know for sure, *you* sure as hell wouldn't get with him."

"Not that you're wrong, but why would you think that?"

"Because he's too old for your chicken-hawk ass."

"Man, I told you I'm leaving the kids alone."

"Yeah, until the next little twentysomething cutie pie crosses your path."

"I don't think so. Not anymore."

"You're serious?"

"You're not the only one looking for love, Bran."

"I guess," Brando mused kindly, amazed but understanding.

And this was the moment. Omar knew it. He could feel it in his bones, in his heart. It was now or never. There was nothing to prevent him. He had to tell him. He opened his mouth to speak, but Brando spoke first.

"You know, it's kind of crazy, but lately, I've been thinking a lot about Collier."

There was a silence only Omar noticed, wide enough for him to look about it and realize he was caught completely off guard, plucked. "Really?" he finally managed to say.

"Yeah," Brando answered with a perkiness previously unknown, while something sank inside of Omar. His chances.

Chapter Forty-three

It was the night before Jeanette Bell was set to testify. Brando gave Jeanette last-minute instructions and warned her that the prosecuting attorney would most likely linger heavily on the lesbian issue, baiting whatever homophobia the jury harbored. He then sent her off to bed early, so that she would be well rested and alert.

But she could not sleep. It was past midnight and she was still sitting up in the bed, in Clymenthia's comforting arms, still wide awake.

"You have to get some sleep, baby," Clymenthia admonished gently.

"I killed a man, Clymenthia." Her words were filled with resignation, her stare at the nothingness across the room regretful.

"You defended yourself."

"But I never thought . . . I never thought that I was capable of ending another human being's life."

"Jen, don't do this to yourself. You have to understand, sweetie, that people die under many, many circumstances—childbirth, old age, accidents, war, natural disasters, being in the wrong place at the wrong time, sickness, broken hearts, criminal activity. We all will die. And very few of us will have a say in how. That man took a chance with his life when he attacked you, and his crimes against you caused his death. He deserved to die, and you were the reluctant instrument used by the universe to make that happen."

"But he was flesh and blood, Clymenthia, a living, breathing being, with a heart and mind, and a wife, a family. Baby, he was somebody's son."

"So was Hitler."

When Jeanette Bell took the stand at 9:38 AM, she seemed rested, alert, and resolved. She found Clymenthia in her regular seat in the courtroom, and returned her partner's nod of confidence with a slight heave that seemed to say, "I'm ready."

Brando's questions were straightforward and uncluttered by emotion. That was deliberate. He was convinced that he would have to sway the jury with truth, not sympathy.

"Did you in any way consent to have sex with Ramon Alexander?" he asked Jeanette while facing the jury.

"No."

"Have you ever had consensual sex with any member of the opposite sex?" he asked, still facing the jury.

"No."

He then approached his client and asked, "In your own words, Jeanette, describe what happened the night Ramon Alexander raped you."

She took a deep breath and prepared herself for the nightmare she would have to relive once again.

In halting but brave words, she recalled waking up from a dizziness on the hood of a car, her hands bound by the strap of her purse, and someone on top of her, and the pain, the excruciating, stinging pain. She told of being thrown to the ground after he raped her, then his retreat toward his car, and then his stopping. He reached for his mouth, discovered the blood, discovered his missing front tooth. Then he turned back to her. She was still on the ground. His eyes were filled with anger as he advanced toward her, cursing and screaming. She tried to scoot away, but he drew closer and closer, angrier and angrier. And then suddenly she remembered the gun in her purse. With all she had left, she struggled to open the purse, fumbled to find the revolver. Her heart beat so hard it felt like tiny rapid explosions. And he still kept on coming. Before she knew it, she had fired the gun. Then again, and again, and again, and again.

At the end of her testimony, she cried. Brando asked for a short recess so his client might recover.

"The court will recess for a half an hour," Judge Stork said. The strike of his gavel broke the silence in the room that shortly thereafter filled with low murmurs.

"Do you like men?" was Marion Madrano's first question when court reconvened.

"What do you mean?" Jeanette asked.

"Like them," the prosecutor continued. "Friendships, cordial acquaintances."

"I have several male friends."

"Several?"

"Some."

"Some. Not several."

"Yes."

"So do you like men?"

"As friends and acquaintances. Yes."

"Have you ever used the term 'breeder'?"

"Yes."

"Specifically, who are you referring to when you use the term 'breeder'?"

"Men."

"What kind of men? Homosexual, heterosexual, bisexual?"

"Heterosexual men."

"If you had to define the term 'breeder' either as a term of endearment or a term of derision, how would you define it?"

"I wouldn't define it as either."

"But if you had to."

"I couldn't say."

"Okay. When, in the past, you've referred to a heterosexual man as a breeder, were you being complimentary?"

"I was making an identification using an acceptable term."

"If I called you a dyke, would that be an acceptable term?"

"An acceptable term for whom?"

"For lesbians."

"Some lesbians have no problem with the term, just like some gay people have no problem with the term 'queer,' and some black people have no problem with the term 'nigger.' Some heterosexual men have no problem with the term 'breeder.' "

"Did you ever refer to Ramon Alexander as a breeder?"

"Yes."

When was the last time you referred to Ramon Alexander as a breeder?"

"Sunday, November twelfth. At Eso Won Books."

"To whom did you refer to him as a breeder?"

"Clymenthia Teager."

"Were you upset at the time you referred to Lieutenant Alexander as a breeder?"

"No, not really."

"When you came back into the storeroom where your lover, Clymenthia Teager, was, did she or did she not ask you what's wrong?"

"She did."

"Would you say that she knows you very well?"

"Yes."

"When she asked you, 'What's wrong?' what did you say?"

Jeanette took a moment, which was a moment too long for Madrano.

"Should I ask the question again, Miss Bell?"

"I said . . . 'Just a little harassment from a damn breeder.' "

Chapter Forty-four

With Brando busy with the trial and new thoughts of Collier, with Shane out of his life, and loveless sex losing its luster, Omar began spending time alone with his memories. Today of all days—June 23—brought the unholy trinity of a saddened heart, an empty soul, and a hating mind back much too vividly. It was the twenty-third anniversary of Grammy's death.

He had lived all his life a motherless child, a fatherless son. That it had not taken an even greater toll on his life was indeed a miracle. And now he was growing weary of the sorrow and the hate, the missing his grandmother, hating his mother, hating himself for missing and hating.

He had all of the trappings but none of the flesh and blood of life well lived. He could write everyone else's story but could not truly face the facts of his own. He did not know the facts; did not want to know them, even though they had glared back at him for a lifetime, pulling his coattail, whispering his name, calling him over, punking him with his own insignificance.

You're nothing to no one. The last person you truly mattered to died twenty-three years ago. No one wants to know your story.

No one wants to know your life. No one wants to know your grief. It's not even worth killing yourself over. Who would care if you died? The magazine editors with writers to spare? The Hollywood publicists who wine and dine yo' invisible ass to get a few inches of ink for some high-paying celebrity client? The God that you're not even sure you believe in? The boys that you bedded and baited with trinkets and cash and trips and good dick they could get anywhere? The track runner? The Silver Lake thug prince? Shane? Who would care? The friends that you never made, the people you were too afraid to get too close to? The resentful women who found you a wanton waste? The fire-and-brimstoners? Who would care?

Brando, maybe.

He bought the flowers at Mrs. Olivera's shop on Centinela and La Brea, just as he always did.

"You go see your Grammy?" the beautiful silver-haired Mexican immigrant asked knowingly, herself a grandmother.

"Yes, ma'am," Omar answered respectfully. He always marveled at those ancient but delicate hands of hers that carefully created and wrapped the mixed bouquet, an order she knew as well as her art.

"She knows how fortunate she is to have you, Omarito," she said softly. "That is why she smiles down on you. That is why you must always smile back."

Omar kept that in mind as he drove down Florence Avenue toward the Inglewood Cemetery. As he passed through the gates, he did manage a smile as he recalled those few years of youthful happiness living with Grammy, believing life with her would last forever. He could see her lovely face smiling back at him as he parked his car at the curb, next to the rolling green.

He got out of his car and stood next to it. Slowly he twirled the bouquet in his hand, then slowly he lowered his nose to it and took in the gardenia and lilac fragrance. Grammy's fragrance.

He looked over the beautiful grounds. Headstones and markings were scattered gently as far as the eye could see, like still-life picnickers basking away under the warm summer sun.

He walked slowly through the well-manicured grass and read the names on the graves that he passed; familiar names, names he had gotten to know over the years. *Edwin Scarborough, 1921–2000, Beloved Husband, Father, and Grandfather. Cecelia Preston, 1898–1979, Rest in Peace. Aaron and Angela Winslow, August 4, 1963–August 5, 1963, Heaven's Children from Now till Eternity.*

Grammy's grave was just over the hill, shaded under a ficus tree a hundred yards in the distance. A warmth filled him as he thought about what they would talk about on this fine day.

As he drew closer, he could make out the headstone, and only that. He did not really notice the figure kneeling down at the grave next to Grammy's. He did, however, notice the fresh flowers on Grammy's grave.

Curiously, he continued his leisurely stroll, then slowly, very slowly, he realized that the figure was not kneeling down at the grave next to Grammy's. The figure, the woman, was kneeling down at Grammy's grave, had placed the fresh flowers there. His curiosity began to get the best of him.

And then it hit him, slowing down his pace, stopping him finally. It had been so long that he hardly recognized her. It was his mother.

He stood there and stared; anger tried to surface, but it was sadness that ultimately lowered his head.

Off to his left was a small cluster of trees. That's where he retreated. He sat on the grass in back of them.

Time had not been good to the woman who gave him birth. Seated uneasily on the ground before Grammy's grave, she was defeated by her slightness, her weariness, her impishness. Omar felt sorry for her.

And she was crying, as much as her frailty would allow. Omar had no idea his mother knew how to cry. Seeing this, he suddenly had an urge to run to her and take her in his arms and maybe even say to her what Mrs. Olivera said to him. *She smiles down on you, Momma, that is why you must always smile back.* But he couldn't . . . he just couldn't.

He waited until she was done, had cried herself out, had struggled to lift herself up off the ground, steadying her ancient body on a cane of no distinction, had managed herself beyond Grammy's grave, had gotten to the distant road and beyond.

He watched her disappear in the distance, even as he slowly made his way to Grammy's grave, where he stood looking off after her for a very long time. Then finally he kneeled down to his grandmother. The flowers his mother had left were beautiful. He placed his mixed bouquet next to them.

That night, he did something he did not think he was capable of doing. He got down on his knees, next to his bed, and prayed to the God he wasn't sure he believed him, and asked him to please remove the hate. *Please, God, please . . .*

Chapter Forty-five

W e all sympathize with what Miss Bell has gone through," Marion Madrano began in her closing statement. "I cannot think of a greater crime against a woman. But we have courts, a judicial system to determine what is to be done with those who commit crimes, after thoroughly establishing that a crime has been committed. Miss Bell set herself up as judge, jury, and executioner. She and she alone determined that Lieutenant Alexander committed a crime, and she and she alone determined that his sentence would be death. And so she killed him, an illegal killing, which makes it murder. She murdered him in cold blood out of revenge for what he had already done to her, not to protect herself against what he might do to her. Many of us, when we think we've been wronged, may feel like killing the person that wronged us. But the law says we cannot. Jeanette Bell ignored the law, and killed him anyway. Jeanette Bell is guilty of murdering Ramon Alexander."

There was a hush in the courtroom when Marion Madrano completed her closing remarks. The sound of her heels clicking on the slat-wood floor echoed against the hallowed walls as she walked back to the prosecution table.

Brando sat at the defense table next to Jeanette and pondered for a moment. He looked into his client's eyes. The silence that they shared spoke volumes. They were in this thing together.

Jeanette's hands were folded on the table, delicate hands. Brando put his hand on hers and squeezed them ever so gently, but confidently. He smiled at her reassuringly. She smiled back, and nodded the go-ahead.

He stood under the expectant eyes of the courtroom—the citizens behind him, the judge, bailiff, and court reporter in front of him, the six men and six women in the jury box to his left. He turned to the jury and slowly approached them. He stood before them, took a deep breath, then exhaled evenly.

"Each one of you has to be Jeanette Bell on that terrible night, for that horror-filled hour," he began. "Each and every one of you has to know the feeling of fighting for your life.

"Jeanette Bell is on trial for defending herself against a violent criminal. If she is guilty, then all of us are guilty each time we defend our wives, our children, our loved ones, God help us, ourselves from a violent criminal attack. Jeanette Bell was being raped by a man who enjoyed hurting women, and when he turned to come back after her, she defended herself. She stopped him the only way she knew how. The rapist was not about to stop himself. How much longer would Jeanette Bell have to suffer if she had not stopped this from happening to her? Would she even be alive today if she had not acted defensively? She not only defended herself, she defended us all, and the constitutional right that we all inalienably possess. For what she has done, we should not convict this courageous woman. We should give her a medal."

* * *

After closing arguments, Judge Stork read a half hour of instructions to the jury, informing them that they had only three verdict choices—guilty of second degree murder, guilty of voluntary manslaughter, or not guilty—and what each verdict would mean.

At 6 PM the jury retired to consider its verdict. Three days later they were still deliberating. But Detective Edetta Franklin did not need to hear a verdict to determine what she had to do. He was still walking around living and breathing as if he had done nothing, as if he had not destroyed another human being, a walking stalking cadaver. He had to know and suffer, so that whatever afterlife he was consigned to would remind him of the sins of his former life revisited at great and painful consequence.

The right or wrong of it did not matter anymore. All that mattered was closure. And now, finally, the motherfucker was dead. She washed the blood off, went home to her husband, and made love to him as she'd never made love to him before.

Finally.

Edetta Franklin was a happy woman. Sometimes you have to just kill something to even the score.

One the fourth day of jury deliberation, the jury informed Judge Stork that they had reached a verdict. Brando received the call with a foreboding that had been building. An overnight verdict in a case like this most likely would have meant that the jury accepted the self-defense argument and that Jeanette killed her attacker justifiably.

Deliberation longer than that was not good news for the defense. There were no rebuttal witnesses to Jeanette's story, yet there were jurors who did not believe she was innocent. The system, ruled by the laws of men, could still lay blame on female rape victims for the defensive death of a male attacker. Statistics had shown this to be the case disproportionately. It was a crapshoot, and Brando knew it.

But still he believed. The defense had spoken nothing but the truth, and he had to depend on that to save Jeanette from going to prison.

He called Jeanette and Clymenthia from his office the moment he got the call.

"We're due in court at one," he told Clymenthia. "I'll pick you up at noon."

"Thanks, Bran."

"How is she doing?"

"She's hanging in there. We both are. We have faith."

"See ya at noon."

Chapter Forty-six

Dee Bohannon rang Selma's doorbell several times. Still there was no answer. She then pulled out her cell phone and dialed Selma's number. Voicemail picked up. She pulled out the key Selma had given her for moments like this. More likely than not, Selma was inside drunk and blacked out (even though it was the middle of the afternoon), a not uncommon state for her, one Dee had gotten used to, though it worried her more and more.

"Sel?" she called out as she opened the door leading into Selma's wide foyer. Still no answer. She shut the door quietly behind her, and in the stillness she heard the familiar grunts and growls of Selma's booze-induced snoring pouring out from behind the slightly ajar door to Selma's media room. She knew she would find her poor drunken friend laid out in a stupor.

Easily she pushed the door open. And there she was. Selma. Sprawled out on the sofa. Saliva dribbled from her mouth, down her neck.

Dee shook her head, pulled out a Kleenex, and dabbed at the mess. Selma did not budge, save for the snoring that blew the stench of stale liquor in Dee's face as she wiped it.

Drinking and watching her gay porn was Selma's great pastime. The drinking Dee could barely keep up with, and did not desire to. The gay porn had become a guilty pleasure for Dee. She and Selma had spent hours viewing and reviewing titles like *Black and Huge, Hot Rod,* and *Ruffneck Workout.* Not only were they erotically thrilling but they provided great education and reaffirming. For Dee, sex with her ex could not have been better, and viewing the experts on-screen reaffirmed that dick sucking and ball licking and salad tossing and taking Kevin's delicious penis in every hole of her body with the greatest of ease and desire were arts she had truly mastered.

So while Selma lay drunk, asleep, and slobbering on the sofa, Dee decided to treat herself. The viewing would be in honor of a wonderful man she could not figure out why she divorced.

Good old Selma. Something was already on top of the machine. Dee picked up the video and read the handwritten label. *Sexy Secret Spycam Special,* it said in Selma's familiar scroll. Dee put it in the machine and hit PLAY on the remote. As the images rolled before her, she was surprised at the poor quality—stagnant and grainy, certainly not up to Selma's spit-polish standards. But what struck Dee—pleased her—was the sweet gentleness of the sex, which was not just mere sex.

Lovemaking.

It was lovemaking. Personal, passionate, and caring lovemaking. Two beautiful black men on-screen kissed and held each other as only lovers would. She smiled as only a person truly touched smiled.

Then her smile froze, and her eyes slowly bulged. At first

she was unable to believe what she saw, but the video dumb-struck her horrifically.

Brando!

Brando on-screen, making love, love so private, so intimate that he in no way could have known he was being filmed. Dee felt like a violator, a vile voyeur, his betrayer. And even as she was getting sick to her stomach, she could not turn her head or run away.

She then realized the remote was still in her hand. It stung, then it stiffened. Robotically she hit POWER.

Standing in the middle of the dark room, she was unable to budge except for a slight tremble that moved quickly through her.

She tried to remove the images from her mind, but could not. The sight of Brando and the man—most assuredly his ex-lover, Collier—played over and over inside her head. She then suddenly remembered something Selma had said: "I've had a set of keys to his house since he moved in. When I first sold him the place. Good neighbor policy." And it all made sick sense.

What had Selma done? What had she done?

Dee's cell phone ringing and vibrating shot through the silence. She flinched.

"Hello?" She answered her phone in a whisper.

"Dee?" A familiar voice asked.

"Brando," she spoke with a forced lightness.

"It's over," he said. "It's over."

Chapter Forty-seven

Although Judge Canton W. Stork had warned the court that any outburst or displays of emotions would not be tolerated at the reading of the verdict, the courtroom exploded into an uproar when the foreman read from the folded paper: "Not guilty."

Jeanette, standing next to Brando, grabbed him and shook him with a glee she had not known since the proceedings began. Clymenthia burst through the docket gates and grabbed the both of them. Tears flew everywhere.

There were few present who disagreed with the verdict. There was Marion Madrano, of course, and even she approached Brando and graciously congratulated him.

And now it was over. Dee congratulated Brando over the phone in a strange voice that he was too paralyzed with excitement and happiness to note. He managed to tell her that he would talk to her later. He had to get back to his client. On the drive home he began planning the victory celebration.

The Jeanette Bell case would become a cautionary tale and a cause célèbre. Halle Berry snapped up the film rights. Brando was, of course, set to broker the deal. He was back to being an entertainment lawyer, though that return to criminal law changed him forever. He did not have to sit on the sidelines of life and miss the passion of life's ups and downs. Instead of watching the parade, he would be in it. He promised himself at least that.

Back home, where he popped champagne before Jeanette and Clymenthia went off to the guest bedroom to celebrate in their own special way, Brando picked up the phone and dialed a number he had not dialed in nearly two years.

"Brando." Collier answered after the second ring.

"How you been?"

"Good. How about you?"

"Great."

"So I've been reading and seeing and hearing."

"Collier, man, it's so good to hear your voice."

"Same here, Brando. Same here."

"Ah, listen. I'm throwing a little victory party for Jeanette early Friday night, around six, before Clymenthia and she head back to Connecticut. Why don't you drop by? She'd love to see you again. They'd love to see you. A lot of people would. Me included."

There was a long pause on the other end. Then finally: "Sure, Brando. I'll be there. Friday night. Six o'clock."

Dee thought on it long and hard. Still, she was not sure what to do about it. The video of Brando and Collier she had seen at Selma's was shocking enough; the idea that Selma had clandestinely filmed them was simply immoral. This act told her more about Selma Fant than she cared to know, and more about herself. She didn't know whether to hate or feel sorry for Selma.

It was the eve of Jeanette Bell's victory party. It would be the first time Dee would encounter both Selma and Brando since seeing the tape, and she wasn't quite sure how she would handle it.

Omar knew that Brando's ex, Collier, was going to be at the party, and it was breaking his heart. If Brando and Collier were getting back together, if there was even the possibility of it, Omar would have no choice but to surrender his romantic desires, which were growing out of control, and settle for the platonic love he and Brando had shared so long; still shared.

For a fleeting moment Omar thought about the track runner and the Silver Lake thug prince, Thomas and Andrew, and for the first time he thought about them as something more than sex partners. Or maybe nothing more than sex partners.

Who knows? Who really knows?

All he knew for sure was that he liked them, genuinely, but was not in love with them. He liked Shane enough to be hurt by him, but he was not in love with him. He had only been in love once. Still was.

On the way to the party he stopped at the Liquor Bank on Stocker and Crenshaw and bought two magnums of Dom Pérignon. One for Jeanette. One for Brando.

Part Three

Chapter Forty-eight

Jazz poured through the grand portals like a gardenia-scented breeze, whispering tales on the sly. Here Brando lived isolated but comfortably. That's how Senior Father felt it in his melodramatic mind when he rang the doorbell at exactly 6 PM. Brando answered with hugs and kisses, but Senior Father sensed scandal in the air.

"So I hear Collier's on the guest list," he purred.

"Yes." Brando beamed unconsciously, leading Senior Father to the kitchen, where Omar was garnishing the hot duck salad.

"Liz and Dick. The second act," said Senior Father.

"Do you know how old you'd have to be to get that?" Omar snapped.

"*You* got it," Senior Father snapped back.

"And how are you this evening?" Omar asked, cracking a smile.

"As fabulous as ever!" Senior Father declared.

"Yes, you are," Omar agreed.

"Damn, that looks good," Brando said, eyeing the beautiful salad arrangement.

"Thanks, Bran." Omar blushed coolly. Brando reached out to sample a piece of hot duck and was rewarded with a terse slap on the hand.

"Let the guests see it first, Brando," Omar reprimanded.

"Sorry." Brando pouted like a little boy lost in the do-not-touch cookie jar.

"My God, the two of you act like lovers," Senior Father mused.

It's no act, Omar thought while Brando smiled.

"So where's our guest of honor?" Senior Father continued, having read Omar's mind and Brando's smile.

"They're getting dressed," Brando answered.

"Good," Senior Father insisted. "This is Jeanette Bell's night. An entrance is essential."

Radar led him to the bar, where he made himself a perfect three-olive Tanqueray martini.

The doorbell rang again and Brando answered it. Selma and Dee were age-before-beauty divas, though the younger, Dee, was less cheerful. Clearly there was something on her mind. Selma was torn up, way ahead of the game, and after obligatory kisses and a pinch of Brando's ass, sonar took her to the bar, where Senior Father lounged, the oldest man she knew, though she was several years his senior.

"Lacey," she sang whiskey-voiced while fixing her drink by touch. She never referred to Lacey Cannon as Senior Father. From her perspective, he was clearly not a senior.

"The diva of Baldwin Hills," he saluted with his cocktail.

"So they say," she lamented as she took her first gulp at this station.

More guests arrived—Brando's parents wearing their

weekend Palm Spring tans, church children dropping in on their way to the clubs, colleagues of Jeanette and Clymenthia, sisters from ULOAH, congregants from Unity Fellowship and First AME, writers and warriors in the cause—and still no Collier. Brando refused to worry and Omar felt a moment's relief.

And then there he was.

Three pairs of eyes picked Collier out of the swarm entering Brando's house. The third set belonged to Dee, who recognized Collier from Brando's sweet reminiscence and Selma's tawdry and scandalous tapes.

Then a swell from the far hallway averted attention, and shrills and applauds erupted and rolled through the house.

Jeanette Bell, on the arm of her partner, seemed tired but jubilant, thinner but stronger. Her smile was graceful and dignified as she embraced the goodwill of the crowd of well-wishers. Senior Father highly approved.

Jeanette and Clymenthia would be taking the red-eye to Boston and then an hour's car ride across the state line, in the next day's new sun, to their farmhouse in the snow-covered countryside of Connecticut. They had not been home in months. This party was a great send-off, a great good-bye, until the next time.

"You made it," Brando said to Collier loudly, over the surrounding jubilance.

"Yeah," Collier answered, accepting Brando's hug, which Omar could not bear.

"Listen, you know your way around," Brando said, reluctantly abandoning Collier for host duties.

"I do, don't I?" Collier said to the air.

"Damn, man, what's it been?" Omar said from behind.

"Hey, Omar," Collier said warmly, recognizing the voice even before he completed the turn. He gave his former best-friend-in-law a hug. "It's been a while. So what have you been up to?"

"Same-o, same-o."

"I see you've been taking care of my boy," Collier said, eyeing Brando smiling and cutting respectfully through the crowd toward the open arms of Jeanette and Clymenthia. "He's looking good, he's looking happy."

"Yeah, well I'm a good babysitter."

"You're a good friend, Omar. He's very lucky."

"Yeah, he is, isn't he?"

A holler went up as the guest of honor and her lady draped their host, then all three clinched fists they held high in the air over smiles of relief, encircled by ovations of pride and respect.

"And the trial." Collier was amazed, touched by the sight of it all. "Damn!"

"He did a great job," Omar agreed. "The next Johnny Cochran. But you knew that already, didn't you?"

"Yeah, I did. I always did. He's quite a guy."

"Yeah, he is."

"Listen to us," Collier then said, "a two-man fan club."

"One of many," Omar said to the air.

From the bar, which he comonitored with a drunk Selma Fant, Senior Father delighted in the body language and readable lips of Brando's two men. He sipped to the sight of it and the irony of it all.

222

Chapter Forty-nine

Eight PM. The party was two hours old. Omar's hot duck salad was a ravaged hit. Two cases of champagne had been consumed festively. Omar's magnums of Dom Pérignon had not been touched yet.

Selma Fant was finally led to the sofa by Dee. The older woman's high was wearing off and Dee was relieved, but still very much disturbed by all that she knew.

"Do you ever wonder why she drinks so much?" Senior Father had eased up on the two women and observed the semi-lucid matron with condescending admiration.

"I'm drunk, you old dowager queen, not deaf," Selma rattled off suddenly from under her slouch.

"And so you are," Senior Father acknowledged with piss-elegant glee. "How's the baby?" He began to dig deeper.

"You should know better than I," Selma answered.

Dee deciphered from the sidelines. Lacey's prowling into this area so sensitive to Selma confirmed for Dee what she had suspected upon first meeting Senior Father Lacey Cannon. She did not like him.

"Please," Lacey responded to Selma's nuanced-filled tiff, "I don't go out much anymore." He continued fleetingly, "No clubs, no drag shows. I only do house parties. In fact, why weren't you at my winter supper?"

"Was I invited?"

"It's every year, Selma. You know you have a standing invitation."

"Perhaps I was not standing at the time."

"Well I hear that Miss Zara—"

"Earl-Anthony."

"—Miss Zara Earl-Anthony is back in town."

"You okay, Selma?" Dee cut in. On more than one occasion, during their drinking confessionals, Selma had told and retold the story of Peter Caise.

"I think it's time for me to go," Selma said.

"I'll see you home," Dee said as she helped Selma up from the couch.

"I'll go with you," Senior Father chimed in slyly.

"Thanks, Lacey, but it's just next door."

"Nonsense, Miss Dee. Two lovely ladies let loose unto the badlands of these black bourgeois hills without proper male escort? I think not."

"Selma, you're not leaving, are you?" Brando appeared out of nowhere.

"I'm feeling a little sick, hon. If I'm going to throw up, I'd rather throw up in my own commode," she lied with a feckless grin. "Give the ladies my regards."

"I will."

"Dee and I will be right back," Senior Father said, opening the front door and escorting Selma out. Dee followed.

"You guys hurry back," Brando said. "Feel better, Selma."

"I will," Selma answered, her voice fading into the night.

Chapter Fifty

Peter Caise took a chance. It was a winter night that grew dark early. When he rang Selma Fant's doorbell it was already pitch-black, save for the porch light and fully lit party next door. And it was a chance. The Baldwin Hills security patrol units would not take lightly to someone unknown in these parts, soliciting at this hour.

He rang the doorbell again. Still no answer. It took everything he had to return to the scene of the crime. But here he was, ready to say he was sorry to both mother and child.

"May I help you?" he heard from behind, the voice of a rather stern man. He turned and looked up into the face of the powerfully effete gentleman, and the face of the woman next to him, and the drunken face of the woman next to her; the woman he'd made love to two decades ago, and it hardly seemed possible.

And then she looked at him, through drunkenness and all. And Selma shivered with recollection in the arms of her stalwart friend Dee.

"Peter Peter Pumpkin Eater." Her words were soft and awestruck, spoken with hardly a slur, spoken slowly to self-convince.

And then Dee knew, suddenly realized. This was the man Selma had hidden in a bottle from all these years. This was the man Selma Fant had spent so many years hating herself for.

Dee felt a sudden haughtiness that placed a barrier between the illicit lovers from the guilty past.

Peter stumbled nervously. "I didn't know any other way to contact you."

Selma looked at him, quizzically, amazed at how much he seemed not to have changed in face and body, yet how different he was from the cocksure teenage sex machine who fucked her and her son, forever enslaving her in a relentless perversity she could not escape, even if she had wanted to.

She tried to feel sorry for him, but all she could do was feel sorry for herself, a vileness rising up inside of her, like the liquor sickness she pretended to have.

All the while, Senior Father stood in the shadows in silence, afraid to disrupt the flow of what was about to be spilled, whatever it was; a gossip's delight.

"Why did you need to see me?" Selma finally managed to get out.

"I need to talk to you."

"Excuse me. Kadidra Dempsey-Bohannon," Dee interjected, extending her free hand.

"Peter Caise." Peter shook her hand politely.

"And this is Mr. Lacey Cannon." Dee exposed Senior Father rudely from the shadows.

"Hello." Lacey spoke in a forced baritone.

"Mr. Cannon," Peter acknowledged with a polite nod.

"If you don't mind, Mr. Caise," Dee continued, "Mrs. Fant

isn't feeling well. You might want to arrange to speak with her at another time."

"It's all right, Dee," Selma interrupted. "Come in, Peter."

Selma seemed surprisingly lucid, given her usual state. Memories of things so hard to forget splashed in her face with a sobering chill as she opened her front door and led Peter in.

She then turned and stopped Dee and Lacey at the threshold.

"Are you sure?" Dee warned, with Lacey concurring.

"I'm very sure," Selma said with a newfound sobriety. "Now go back and enjoy the party."

It all came painfully back to Peter. The staircase to the bedrooms. Making love to Earl-Anthony because he thought that he loved him; making love to Earl-Anthony's mother for the cleansing he needed for thinking he loved a man. And as sad as it all seemed, he had to chuckle a bit inside, at the absurdity of it all, the absurdity that causes mere man to question the nature that God has assigned. And so for this he needed to apologize; for succumbing to the absurdities of mere mortal man, and seducing two others in his self-loathing acts.

He did not feel nervous anymore as Selma offered him a seat in the living room. He declined the cocktail she offered. Oddly, she did not make a drink for herself.

Neither knew just how to begin or within whose court the ball was in. They both accepted blame. And they both needed to hear it from the only other person who could say it from truth. It never should have happened.

But before all of that, and for a very long time, they sat in silence.

Chapter Fifty-one

B y the way, I thought you might want to take a look at this," Brando said, handing Clymenthia the document. "The deal with New Line."

"Thanks, Bran," she said with a cursory glance at the papers in hand, handing them to Jeanette, who sat snuggled up to her.

"You're welcome," he answered, kissing her gently on the cheek.

"For everything," Jeanette said. Her eyes then smiled up at him, gratefully.

The party had been a rousing success, filled with unexpected moments of poignancy and self-reflection. And now it was almost over. It was the final farewell to an ordeal that would forever change the lives of Jeanette Bell and Clymenthia Teager.

It was something that Clymenthia Teager would eventually write about and Jeanette Bell would lecture on. Within that vast love that Clymenthia had for Jeanette was a deep admiration, deepened by events that no one should endure. And Jeanette Bell was living proof of the infallibility of the soul, its indestructibility.

"I'm going to talk about this," she said. "Hopefully get other people talking."

What was not being talked about across the room was the mysterious young man at Selma's door, a presence that sobered the old girl up like voltage. Getting anything out of Dee Bohannon was hopeless. Senior Father Lacey Cannon was at his wit's end.

"Why are you acting like you don't know anything when I know you know something?" he accused with jovial impatience, following Dee into Brando's kitchen, rendering her escape futile.

"Wrong, Lacey," Dee defended with a sigh, retrieving a bottle of Perrier from the refrigerator. "And anyway, you don't know me that well and I don't like you that well, even if I knew anything."

"Ah, excuse me?"

"You're a vicious little stereotype. Now, if you'll excuse *me*."

She brushed past him and rejoined what was left of the party. Senior Father Lacey Cannon made a mental note. Dee Dempsey-Bohannon would not be added to the guest list of next year's winter supper.

Andrew, the Silver Lake thug prince, was still up and willing when Omar made the call. The attempted attitude prompted by Omar's long absence soon fizzled with the prospect of some fucking. It had been months, and oh how he missed all that thick senior dick.

Omar had left the party early, finding it hard to stand by

and witness the pining that seemed to transmit back and forth between Brando and Collier. Always the good friend to the end, Brando tried to convince Omar to stay, but Omar begged off with some lame excuse, a suddenly remembered deadline he'd forgotten. Omar was angry with himself for not speaking up for what was in his heart.

He pulled over to the curb and turned off the engine. He sat there a long time. And then he decided. He flipped open his cell phone and hit SPEED DIAL.

"Hey," said the Silver Lake thug prince.

"Hey, man," Omar said, his voice coolly lowered.

"Hey," the Silver Lake thug prince answered back again, gently caressing his balls with anticipation.

"Listen, man . . . Listen."

"Yeah?"

"I can't make it tonight."

"What?" He stopped caressing his balls and froze.

"I suddenly remembered."

"What?"

"I'm under a deadline."

Chapter Fifty-two

I t was as if time had stood still—Collier in the kitchen load-
ing dishes into the dishwasher while Brando vacuumed
the hardwood floors. They seemed the perfect couple in perfect
afterparty mode. They cleaned and they laughed like old
friends and lovers glad to be around each other and in their old
routine.

Oh, the fantasies that danced inside Brando's head.

The party wrapped around midnight, an hour after the car
service had picked up Jeanette and Clymenthia and whisked
them off to LAX for the red-eye flight back home. And now it
was just Brando and Collier, Collier and Brando. It was the
first time all night the former mates had a chance to be alone together, and for Brando it seemed oh-so-familiar, yet oh-so-
new.

With their chores finished, they plopped down on the sofa
in the living room. Vintage Luther hummed softly in the back-
ground.

"She was very lucky to have you, Bran. You're a very good
litigator," Collier said, sipping his coffee. "Remember, I
know."

"You remember better than I do." Brando laughed.

"Please. You wear innocence a lot better than modesty."

Brando recognized that sparkle in Collier's eyes.

"You're a good criminal defense lawyer, Bran. And you know it. I'm just glad you grew the balls back to practice what you know. God don't like waste."

"I think I've grown balls to do a lot of things."

"Really?"

"I called *you*, didn't I?"

"It didn't take balls to do that."

"Yes it did, Collier. I couldn't have done it before now. Not with what I have to say to you. I want to try again; this time, *really* try. I want us to be back together, Collier. I want to be back in your life, share your life. I want you to share mine."

In the back of his mind, Collier knew this was coming, and it scared him; the not knowing how to react, the not knowing what to say, or how to say what he had to say. He took another sip of coffee, a thoughtful sip. And then the words came to him.

"If we couldn't make it in ten years, what makes you think we could make it now?"

"I love you," Brando said, not missing a beat, startling himself. Collier was startled as well, disturbed by the words that he heard. "I love you," Brando said again. "I love you, Collier."

Collier took a breath, then one more sip of coffee. "I've waited so long to hear you say that," he said.

"And I mean it."

"I know you do, but—"

"But what?"

"It's too late for us, Bran."

"What?"

"It's too late."

"No. No it's not."

"Yes it is."

"Why?"

"I'm involved with someone."

Brando couldn't speak. The sensation dizzied him with a heaving he had not experienced since back in the day when Earl-Anthony broke his teenage heart.

"Did you expect me to just sit around and wait for you to have this epiphany?" Collier asked as kindly as he could.

"When . . . when did this, ah . . . when did this happen?"

"It's very new. We met about a month ago . . . at one of 'those meetings' you always hated going to. An empowerment group for black gay men."

"One of those vent sessions."

"You should try venting sometimes, Brando. It might do you some good."

"So where is this new Mr. Right?" Brando asked with more acid than intended.

"He's a navy guy, stationed at Camp Pendleton down in San Diego."

"Is it real?"

"That's what I'm hoping."

"So why did you come here tonight?"

"You invited me."

"But you should have known—"

"I didn't know anything. All the years we were together, I didn't know anything."

"Was it ever good?"

"It was never bad, Bran. It was just never on fire."

"I've been celibate two years, Coll! Two years, waiting for you!"

"I thought about not coming. But then I had to come, and finalize things. I was so proud of you when I saw you in the courtroom doing your thing. I thought that maybe finally you had rediscovered some passion in your life."

"I did, I have!"

"Then share it with somebody. And when you do find that person, don't wait ten years to tell them that you love them."

Collier took a final sip of coffee. He set the cup down on the coffee table and stood before Brando, who was seated and weakened by the blindsiding. He reached down to him and brought him up out of the chair. Then he hugged him, in a hug that said good-bye.

For the first time in a long time Brando could not sleep soundly. All night long he tossed and turned. What he had built up in this newly opened mind and this newly opened heart came pouring out with a stinging so fierce and so foreign that his eyes watered, and his head swung back and forth on his damp pillow, waking him constantly with his own pained shrills.

He sat straight up in bed and he prayed, "Why, dear God, why?" And then suddenly he wanted to curse Collier for cutting so deeply. Then quickly he asked God's forgiveness for cursing a man who had only spoken the bittersweet truth. He had waited too long, stood to the side while life, thorny and funky and jagged and twisted and bitter and sweet, partied on.

Chapter Fifty-three

W e're seeing Miss Zara tonight, don't forget. I'll pick you up at eleven." It was half past noon when Brando checked his voicemail. He had been numb and had ignored the ringing phone. The magnum of Dom Pérignon lay sweating in a bucket of half-watered ice. He needed a drink. He popped the cork and drank from the bottle.

Those last moments with Collier flashed like lightning through the fog in his head. He was losing it all over again.

And then suddenly he heard the echo of Omar's voice. The voicemail. Miss Zara tonight. Collier gone. He drank from the bottle again. And again. And again.

He was sick of himself and his Goody Two Shoes existence. The wild Santa Ana winds rule, like the ones that sparked last winter's Malibu fires. Gentle breezes do nothing, spark nothing. He needed to set something on fire, set himself on fire, not just blow a flower into a smile but torch his soul into feeling; feelings.

But what was this he was feeling now? He was crazy out of his head with self-pity and self-scorn.

"Was it ever good?" he remembered asking stupidly.

It was never bad, Brando. It was just never on fire.

Truth hurts, and he winced at the pain.

He couldn't hold it in any longer. He had to talk to somebody, but not just anybody. He dialed Omar's number. Omar picked up on the second ring.

"You got my message?"

"Yeah."

"So, ah, how did everything go?"

Brando then hesitated, knowing too well what Omar was asking, caught between confession and denial, wanting to blurt it all out and bite down on his tongue at the same time.

"What?" he finally coughed up.

"You and Collier."

He hesitated; faked another cough. Then: "Aw, man, it's . . . it's the beginning of something, you know?" He was a terrible liar, an even worse actor.

"You been drinking, Brando?"

"Still celebrating." The intended chuckle was bogus.

"You okay?"

"Yeah, yeah." He lied again.

"Okay," Omar conceded with hesitance. "So we're still on for tonight, right?"

"Most def'nitely."

"All right, most def'nitely."

"O?"

"Yeah?"

Brando hesitated again, then chickened out. "See ya tonight," he finally said.

"All right, man," Omar answered, trying to make it all out. "See ya tonight. Eleven."

"Eleven."

Brando hung up the phone and drank again from the magnum.

Fuck it, he thought to himself. He was ready for anything, anything to make him forget he had nothing. He pulled out the card she had given him, and dialed the fucking number.

"Brando Heywood," she declared with a sultry cool.

"Hello," Brando responded, disguising his despair, "I thought I'd check and see what you and William were up to."

Chapter Fifty-four

Selma Fant had not moved. It was fortuitous that the rolling liquor cart was in reach. She needn't move to fix the drink after drink she drank through the night, morning, and now afternoon. And still, her misery would not drown. It bore a thousand cuts and would not die. The agony was insurmountable.

Seeing him again, standing at her front door, gave her a heaving she did not want to experience. Desire and disdain twitched with the need to be cleansed, and the dirt nearly won out. She fought the urges that confirmed her sickness, and held herself at bay and never looked below his neck when finally they exchanged "I'm sorry's."

She told him to find his way out and held her head high and eyes straight ahead so that she would not look upon the firm young ass that slowly headed toward the exit. For what seemed an eternity, she did not squeeze the lips between her legs that dripped with moist want.

She fought the urge for as long as she could. And then she grabbed the arms of the Queen Anne chair she sat in and held herself bolted down, not allowing herself to run out of the room and have at him before he got away.

And so all night, and morning, and now afternoon, she sat bolted in that chair, within reach of her liquor, and she drank and she drank, until she could drink no more.

The drive was a short one from Ledera to Don Pedro Drive. It was the preparation that took most of the time. Vanessa and William Ellerbee had both freshly douched, bathed in bath oils, and given each other a drill sergeant's once-over, first impressions being crucial.

It was 3:30 PM when they walked out the door. This evening was a new beginning of old pleasures for them. This evening would be dedicated to the memory of the late DuPré Dixon.

Dee left a message on Selma's voicemail letting her know she was running late. She figured that Selma wasn't picking up because she was probably watching her videos, that video. Dee could not wipe the thought of the video out of her mind, and Selma enjoying it. She thought about it all through the ride to Don Pedro Drive. Should she confront Selma, or should she just leave it alone? She was conflicted and thrown off her game.

At ten of four Peter Caise pulled out of the parking structure of his Park La Brea apartment complex. He was grateful for the red light that held him at the corner of Wilshire and Curson. To his right were the La Brea Tar Pits, and beyond that the L.A. County Art Museum.

He sat there in the light traffic, not sure how he felt. Last night's meeting with Selma Fant was a relief, and yet . . . He could see in Selma's eyes the damage he had done, the damage mutually afflicted. After all those years there was a hunger still in her ancient eyes, a hunger he did not want to satisfy. He could see in her eyes, even as she said that she had forgiven him, that she had not forgiven herself, and was still infirm with damning desire.

The car in back of him beeped its horn politely. The light had turned green. Peter looked up, waved his apology to the rearview mirror, and moved on. After all, he said what he had come to say to Selma Fant. The demons were no longer shared. He had dealt as best he could with his. She would have to do the same.

Move on.

He drove east on Wilshire and would turn right on Crenshaw. Earl-Anthony, Miss Zara, would be performing later tonight at the Catch One. A special midnight show.

She was now at her sound check. He had called the Catch earlier and found out as much. It was now or never. He was halfway there, halfway to, hopefully, his soul's freedom.

At 4:18 PM Vanessa and William Ellerbee rang Brando's doorbell. Anticipation was heightened as a response seemed interminable.

The door finally opened, revealing a handsome but blurry-eyed Brando. He had willed himself past his tentativeness. He was bolstered by champagne. They exchanged innuendo-laced pleasantries at the door, then he ushered them in with a forced smile and a gesture.

"We're so happy that you called," Vanessa said as she led William in.

"Glad you could make it." Brando spoke softly.

"What a lovely home." Vanessa oohed and aahed while William scanned Brando's body with anxious eyes.

"Thanks. Please, make yourselves comfortable. Would you like a drink?" Brando asked as he led them into the living room.

"Maybe afterward," William said, wasting no time.

"So, how about the grand tour?" Vanessa intercepted.

"Sure," Brando responded. "Right this way. Let's see. Why don't we start with the kitchen?"

"Why don't we start with the bedroom?" William was dead serious.

At a quarter to five Dee pulled into Selma's driveway and parked. She rang the doorbell. There was no answer. She twisted the doorknob. She used her "Selma's drunk" key. She walked in and called out, "Sel?" The echo was followed by silence.

Her heels clicked against the marble foyer as she crossed toward the dim living room light.

She looked in. All was still, museumlike, so still that she did not immediately notice Selma sitting in the Queen Anne, slouching but firmly holding the antique chair's filigree arms.

Dee jumped at the sight of her, was startled by her *boo* presence.

"Girl, you about scared the living daylights out of me." Dee chuckled breathlessly.

But Selma said not a word, budged not an inch. The rolling bar cart was at arm's length, yet Selma's hand was empty. Dee scanned the tableau vivant.

A cocktail glass lay on its side, at Selma's feet, its contents spilled, her expensive Ferragamos soaked, ruined.

"Selma," Dee scolded as she bent down to pick up the glass. "You really need to slow your roll." She fussed as she lifted herself up.

At first she did not realize it, but when she found herself eye to eye with Selma Fant, she knew.

"Selma!" she commanded. She stared deeply into the lifeless eyes, and then she panicked. She shook the limp body with a fury, suddenly, assertively, refusing to accept the inevitable.

"Selma! Selma!" she cried, but Selma would not move on her own, ever again.

And then Dee surrendered, grimly, conceding that she had no choice in the sad matter.

She plopped down on the sofa across from her dead friend. A great sadness preceded reason. She would call the police, in time. She would call Brando, in time. But for now she needed to finish her crying, and pull it together, think it all out, for before she called anyone there was something else she needed to do. It was the least she could do for her friend.

Chapter Fifty-five

For Brando, it was the strangest sensation. He had not been kissed erotically in over two years, and he responded ever-so-slightly to the bitter taste of tobacco on William's breath.

Vanessa leaned forward from her vantage point, a chair in the corner of the room. She held her breath as she watched her husband slowly unbutton Brando's shirt. William slowly peeled down the linen garment, revealing Brando's lean and well-toned torso, modestly rippled.

Brando tried to relax. His nipples stiffened. William took this as a sign. He kissed each one, tongue-circled them moistly, and shivered at the taste of them.

Brando shivered, too, shivered at the memory of Collier, at the memory of Earl-Anthony, even Omar. He had not even noticed that William had shed his shirt as well and had unbuckled his belt. The sound of William unzipping his pants distracted Brando from his sad reverie, and he looked toward the sound just for a moment, only long enough to see William's pants drop to the floor.

William's throbbing erection burst from the slit of his boxers, but Brando's eyes were too blurred to see.

Vanessa's eyes had glazed, too. The vision before her was sad, sweet, and gleeful. Anticipating this innocent and blurry-eyed beauty fucking her man filled her with a wanting she could barely contain.

William slowly fell to his knees, as if to pray, drawing Vanessa to her feet. Silent hosannas rumbled through her breasts.

William's delicate hands found Brando's belt buckle and Vanessa held her breath. As William began to undo the belt, he looked up at Brando, as if to ask permission. But Brando's face, staring straight ahead now, was strangely distant, alluringly so, in need of seduction. William was ready to oblige.

William released the belt, then touched himself in his squatted position. Jizzum juice dripped from his dick, streaking the floor. He brushed his face gently against Brando's soft bulge. William's eyes fluttered and his dick-happy asshole puckered with the need of a fill-up.

He then licked at the hidden bulge that had not changed; played around its cloth covering with a tongue that spoke sign language and touch.

His teeth took hold of the zipper and pulled it down slowly, so slowly his wife could not stand it. She crept up behind him nervously. She looked down on him and realized what she had. She then looked into Brando's distant, unreadable, glistening eyes, and realized she had nothing to fear. When it was all over, her man would be safely returned to her and ready to service the part of her that he could.

"You're a fucking idiot," she heard that son-of-a-bitch Omar say in her head. "And leave my man alone."

But who's the fucking idiot now! And whose man is he

now! Her man. Her man's man. She knew from Brando's blank stare that all she'd have to do is wait her turn.

"No," she then thought she heard.

"No." William thought he heard it, too, but knew he was mistaken. He was this close to heaven. This beautiful man's beautiful dick and beautiful balls, a soft bulge hidden behind Calvin Klein briefs, was right in the palm of his hand, saying yes.

"I can't do this," Brando continued in almost a whisper, brushing William's caressing hand away. "I'm sorry."

William looked up with a shock. Vanessa was still frozen in her slow state of disbelief.

"Sorry?" Vanessa finally managed to ask.

"Oh no, motherfucker, you're gonna do this." William was suddenly standing in Brando's face.

And then it all came back to Brando. Nothing would be taken from him that he was not willing to give. He thought about Jeanette. He thought about Clymenthia. He thought about the pathetic thing he was about to do.

He was eye-to-eye with William. "No," he said again, simply, forthrightly.

Vanessa saw something in Brando's eyes that even William, eye-to-eye, could not see. She reached out to her naked husband, grabbed his arm, and pulled him toward her, out of fear of the unknown. William's penis retreated as well, shriveled in disappointment. He jerked away from his wife and angrily climbed into his jizzum-stained boxers, almost stumbling in the process. He continued to dress in fuming silence.

"Are you sure about this?" Vanessa asked calmly.

"Yes," Brando answered, buttoning his shirt. "I am. I'm sorry."

"We all are. Maybe some other time."

"I don't think so."

Brando led Vanessa and William to the front door and bade them good-bye. He watched through the window as they drove off. He had no regrets, except that maybe he could have loved Collier more, loved Collier deeper.

The champagne magnum sat on the kitchen counter half full, Omar's congratulatory gift.

Omar.

The sudden thought of his friend gave him a warmth he had not felt all day. And he knew that life would go on, would have to, and that perhaps the absence of true love, a void that both men shared, would be filled with the friendship that both of them shared, an enduring friendship. Brando tried to make himself believe what his heart knew was bogus.

He started to take a drink, but realized he'd had enough.

The doorbell rang. *What part of "no" did they not understand?* he thought to himself. He went to the door and opened it.

"Brando," Dee said grimly.

Chapter Fifty-six

Peter stood quietly back in the shadows of the club and stared at her in awe. Miss Zara's beauty in person had not been and could never be justly captured in photos. That she was so breathtaking was of no great surprise. She was born from a breathtaking young man. Even in jeans, heels, and a simple white blouse, she was stunning up there on that stage, and the voice still unforgettable. Peter hung on every word that she sang, while a trio of musicians played softly, worshipfully, behind her.

> To know what it's like
> To hold stardust in your hand
> To see in the night
> When the moonlight says you can
> The brush of a breeze out of nowhere
> Comes and goes
> The comforting waves never stay
> They come and go

He did not know how, but was drawn slowly from the shadows by the melodious haunting, by her spell, by her song, and he knew why he once loved Earl-Anthony even when he did not fully love himself. He thought about how much he must have hurt him, hurt himself, was still hurt.

> Better to have loved and lost they say
> I cannot agree
> For to love is not to lose
> And when I'm old and gray
> My once-upon-a-times
> Will be filled with thoughts of you
> I am stronger now
> I no longer doubt
> What I'm made of
> For I know
> What it's like
> To have loved

"That was beautiful, baby," said Eli, the man she had been singing to. He then stepped up on the stage and kissed her gently. It was a beautiful moment to witness, and Peter's smile caught the single tear that fell.

Eli then turned toward the sound engineer. They exchanged thumbs-ups. "Good job, fellas," he said to the musicians. "I think we got it."

The lovers then exchanged more words, in whispers, and kissed again before parting—he to the sound engineer, awaiting further instructions, she down the stage, onto the dance floor, toward the baby grand piano, where she sat.

Her long, delicate fingers gently picked out the melody

of the song she had just sung. She savored its beauty, and closed her eyes and hummed along. When slowly she opened her eyes, she saw him, for the first time in almost twenty years.

"Peter?" she said with surprised but friendly eyes.

"Earl-Anthony," he said without thinking. He was thrown by the beauty up close, as ravishing in its mystical and timeless female form as it was in its male youth.

"Zara. Miss Zara," she gently corrected.

"Miss Zara," he repeated obediently, ill prepared for the reverence that swelled deep inside. "It's been a long time," he finally continued in almost a stutter.

"Yes it has, hasn't it?"

"You're beautiful. Why am I not surprised?"

"Thank you. So what brings you back to L.A.?"

"I missed home," he said, relaxing a bit, by her cordial liege. "Miss Zara?"

"Yes, Peter?"

Peter knew what he had to say and did not want to be distracted from his mission by small talk and shame.

"About what happened . . . what your mother and I did. What *I* did—was terrible. I am so very sorry. Could you ever forgive me?"

"Hon, I forgave you years ago." And even as those true words left her lips, she, a split second after, wondered why she had forgiven him so easily and still had not been able to forgive her own mother. Why had she been holding on to this self-pity and martyrdom, punishing herself and her mother for what had happened so long ago? How could she free Peter of his burden and leave her mother and herself shackled, respectively, with blame and self-appointed sainthood?

She clutched herself, seeing the clear and simple truth for the very first time, and the self-revelation startled her. She tossed her weave back and then tussled it forward, and she heaved with bulging, glistening eyes, like a church girl dumb-struck by spirit.

She then looked up at Peter, as if seeing him for the first time. And all she could think to do was to kiss his big question-ing lips. And so she rose from the piano and did. His eyes wid-ened in shock and appreciation.

"Thank you, Peter," she then said to him, his face still a headlight-deer cuddly bear in the gentle embrace of her hands. She then called out to Eli, who appeared out of nowhere.

"I gotta make a run, baby," she said to him, giving him a reassuring kiss and hug. "I'll be back in time for the show."

She dashed through the club as everything inside her cried, but she could not cry outwardly. Not right now. Not yet.

She raced down Crenshaw Boulevard and thought about all of the years she existed as a motherless child. Her car auto-matically turned on Stocker Avenue and took her up the hill she had not climbed in years. On Don Pedro Drive she turned, a street she grew up on, first made love on, first had her heart broken on, and she saw the house, just as she remembered it, her home, a place that she missed as much as her parents.

And there were the neighbors she had not seen in years, out on their lawns, their quizzical gazes and hands to their mouths aimed at the place she was heading.

And then past the crowd she saw the ambulance, parked out in front of her family home.

Brando and Dee, holding each other, watched grimly from the Fant driveway as Miss Zara pulled in. They looked up. Brando rushed to Zara getting out of her car while Dee looked on.

"Zara." He held her.

"What's going on, Brando?" she asked, new panic in her voice.

"It's your mother."

"What?"

"I'm so sorry."

"What?" she asked again, unable to believe what she had heard, not wanting to, not wanting to see the paramedics exit the house with a gurney between them, afraid to look under the sheet at the body, and then afraid not to.

She broke free of Brando and halted the gurney. "Is this my mother? Is this my mother?" she heard herself screaming in a voice she had not heard in nearly twenty-odd years.

The paramedics stepped aside respectfully. Miss Zara tore back the sheet and stared down and answered her question; stared down at the still face of her mother. She marveled at the sight, then lost control of her all.

"I'm so sorry, Momma." She sobbed like a child as she rested her head on her mother's cold breasts. "I'm so sorry, Momma. I'm so sorry." She then felt arms surround her, holding her, and believed that her impossible prayer had been answered, that she was in her mother's sweet embrace once again.

But the arms were not her mother's arms.

"Zara," Brando said softly, gently pulling her away and holding her. She turned in his arms and looked into his eyes. She was lost to her surroundings.

And then recognition returned, and realization. She was now truly and totally a motherless child. A new sudden burst of tears could not flood away that devastating truth. Brando's sad and sympathetic eyes could not ease its pain. She collapsed in his arms and let the flood flow.

Chapter Fifty-seven

Eli arrived twenty minutes after receiving the call from Brando.

"Where is she?" he asked urgently when Brando answered the front door.

"In the back," Brando said solemnly. "This way."

Dee, brewing coffee in the kitchen, saw the sturdy man pass through the house behind Brando. She knew that Miss Zara would be in good hands.

Dee thought about her ex, Kevin.

Brando's guest bedroom was darkened by the drawn curtains. The darkness allowed Miss Zara to mourn without holding back.

But it was too little too late. She would never be able to say to her mother what should have been said a long time ago. She was weakened by her guilt and bad timing.

"Baby?" came the soft baritone voice just outside the room. Slowly, the door opened. The sight of Eli, silhouetted by the hall light, caused the tears to gush. He went to her and held her.

"I didn't have a chance to say good-bye," she cried. "I didn't have a chance to say I'm sorry."

He let her cry in his arms. Brando, standing in the hallway, quietly pulled the door shut.

"Miss Zara, this is Omar. I just heard the news on the radio. I am so sorry for your loss. Please let me know if there's anything I can do."

Omar hung up his cell and could only imagine what Miss Zara was going through. He then called Brando.

"Hey, O," Brando answered quietly, noting the caller ID.

"Hey. I just heard about Selma Fant. It's all over the news."

"Yeah, it's terrible, man."

"I tried to reach Miss Zara."

"She's here. She took it pretty hard. She's in the back with Eli."

"Good. She's lucky to have somebody like that."

"Yeah," Brando said softly. He then looked up and saw Eli entering the room. "Hold up, Omar. How is she?" Brando then asked Eli.

"As well as can be expected," Eli answered. "I'm going to take her home. I need to call the club and cancel tonight's show."

"No," Miss Zara said from the doorway of the guestroom. I need to do the show tonight."

"Are you sure, baby?"

"Yes."

"Zara, Omar's on the phone," Brando said. "You feel up to talking?"

"Thanks, Brando. I'll take it." She took the phone from Brando. "Hi, Omar," she said.

"Oh, Miss Zara, I am so sorry."

"Thank you. You *are* coming to the show tonight?"

"Do you think that's such a good idea? I mean, considering what you've gone through?"

"I didn't get a chance to say good-bye to her. I'm going to say it tonight, the best way I know how."

"Then I'll be there."

"You better."

Chapter Fifty-eight

The death of the late councilman's wife was reported throughout the city. So many calls came in to Catch One that management recorded an outgoing message: "In spite of the tragic circumstances that have befallen Miss Zara, she has insisted on going on with tonight's midnight performance. The show will be dedicated to Miss Zara's late mother, Mrs. Selma Fant."

That Miss Zara was onstage performing some six hours after discovering her mother's death perplexed some, while others understood. Her strength in the face of so grave a tragedy was heard in song after song, and many in the overflow crowd were profoundly moved.

Omar thought about his own mother and the schism that existed between them, two stubborn souls forever estranged by the pain they both shared and, perhaps, both inflicted.

But seeing her at the cemetery brought forth a new sadness that had little to do with what he felt he had suffered at the hands of her evangelical denunciations and rejection. The once stalwart and unforgiving wall of a woman had been diminished by time and God knows what else. She was a mere shadow of her holier-than-thou former self, prostrated before her own mother's grave, weakened by tears and perhaps decisions she might have regretted, regret that could never return loved ones to the barely living.

Grammy.

The sudden thought of his grandmother sent a pang through him that threatened to make him hate anew, and so he put Grammy out of his mind so that he could remove his mother from that place where no child should ever place a mother. He felt sorry for her, which means he thought about her. And he wondered if she ever thought about him.

> To know what it's like
> To hold stardust in your hand
> To see in the night
> when the moonlight says you can

To know a mother's love.

There were tears all around him and yet he could not cry. He did not have the capacity to completely feel sorry for himself, at least not to the point of tears.

But he felt Miss Zara, up on that stage, singing her heart out. What he and she shared as too-soon-weaned-off offspring could not be understood by anyone who had not been there.

It was an emptiness, an emptiness that could not even be bettered by the man sitting next to him, who he also did not have. He was motherless and not loved by the one and only man he truly loved; not loved the way he wanted to be, needed to be.

Brando.

As Miss Zara closed her show with her signature song, "I Who Have Nothing," she, too, thought about all that she had lost and who she was, orphaned and unreconciled.

But she refused to suffer long. Mourn, yes, but suffer? She made the choice. She chose life over death, and she would be stronger for it, better for it, because she still had something great and wonderful. She had Eli.

She looked over at him in the wings. They shared that secret smile that only they understood.

She was not without family. Family is not always biological. Family is about who loves you and who you love in return. Somewhere in the Bible it is written that you leave your mother and father and go with your mate, and you create a new family.

"It is not I who have nothing. It is I who have everything."

The crowd shot to their feet and exploded with cheers and applause, saluting her brilliant finale. And she stood there, taking it all in, gratefully, looking from them to the heavens, tears streaking her face as she reached up to God, thanking him for the lessons and strength.

The crowd stomped and bombarded the stage with tens and twenties that descended around her like New Year's Eve confetti. She thanked them graciously and gratefully with arms raised with a humility that only true royals understand.

She then extended her right hand to the wings and urged shy Eli out on the stage. With a little boy's smile, he obliged. The spotlight followed as she met him halfway. Then she kissed him and hugged him and let the world know that *this* was her strength.

"God is love!" she declared. "And love is for everyone!"

The roar of the crowd approved mightily.

Omar was caught up like everyone else. He was up on his feet, flailing his arms, calling Miss Zara's name, dancing quick church steps that came out of nowhere. He was feeling it stronger than ever before. "God is love!" he kept hearing, the chant growing stronger. "God is love!" He joined in, chanting loudly and freely. "And love is for everyone!" There was no holding back now. "Love is for everyone! This was the moment; nothing else mattered. *Love is for everyone!*" he said and praised, filled with the glorious fury. So he turned to Brando and started to tell him.

But Brando was still seated, submerged in this human sea, shaking and trembling with the manifestation that all that surrounded him made it so clear what he did not have. *Love is for everyone,* Brando's heart was telling him. *Love is for everyone . . . but me.*

He was crying as Omar had never seen him cry before, and Omar, panicked, reached for him. But Brando pulled away, stood up quickly, then fought his way through the joy-filled crowd.

Omar rushed right after him, worried and determined, but Brando's pain was too mighty. Omar lost sight of him until he saw his figure dash through the neon-lit exit.

The mist in the air caused the club's moonlit parking lot to sparkle. Brando burst from the club. His sobbing had now become wails, and the wall of the building he leaned against seemed barely able to hold him up.

Moments later, Omar came through the doorway, perplexed and worried. Frantically, he looked around for Brando, who was nowhere in sight. Then he heard the sound of the crying. He found Brando sobbing against the back wall of the building. He rushed to him, grabbed him, and forced him to look at him, but Brando could barely lift up his head.

Brando then suddenly buried his face in his best friend's chest and held him so tightly that neither could breathe.

Somehow in the downpour of sorrow and tears, Brando confessed the truth about what happened with Collier. He cried about being on the outside looking in. He cried for the chance to feel love as he'd never felt it before, with its entire maddening and magnificent all.

And while Brando cried questioningly in Omar's arms, Omar opened his resolute heart and then said, "Close your eyes and listen."

And then he said it. Omar said it. For the first time in his life he spoke the searing thought that had enraptured him with torture for years.

"I love you, Brando," he said. "I love you."

Brando looked up from the fog of his tears and his sorrow. He saw in his best friend's eyes what was always there. And he, strangely, inexplicably, began to feel something that he could not explain but that for some reason needed no explanation. It was as if a long-ignored thorn had been pulled from his aching heart, and the pain was slowly subsiding.

"I've always loved you, Brando."

And suddenly, Brando had no trouble saying it, too. It burst out of him, flowed out of him, like the new tears that began to stream his face. "I love you, too . . . I love you, too.

He grabbed Omar's face and kissed him so hard that they almost tumbled, but they caught each other, held each other, saved each other. They laughed, wildly, and they kissed as if there was no tomorrow.

The full moon smiled down on them approvingly.

Chapter Fifty-nine

It was First Sunday's second service and everyone could tell that there was something different about Brando. Actually, many of his fellow congregants had been bearing witness to the steady transformation that began somewhere around the trial of Jeanette Bell and steadily escalated. The nice-enough guy with the decent-enough heart seemed no longer right there in the middle. Brando Heywood seemed caught up in something wonderful and lilting that perhaps he could not even explain.

At the First Sunday's second service, seated in his usual aisle-end place in the third pew, he could feel his spirit rising as it had never risen before, and his heart was singing in the gospel name a wild and raucous melody he did not recognize, singing loudly from an inner flame, singing for the goodness and the glory of this new and wondrous feeling, created by a God who gave this gift of pleasure, spirit, and commitment freely and abundantly.

Inside his mind, inside his heart, he twisted and turned until he could hold it back no more.

He suddenly found himself shimmying. And then, as if possessed by something heavenly, he threw back his head and threw it forward. Tambourines and voices sounded all around him.

And then it happened. For the first time in his life, in all the wonderful years of his churchgoing life, he was shouting! And when it did happen, it did not even frighten him as he thought it would if he had not been so caught up, if he was his former practical, lucid, standing-on-the-sidelines self. He found himself shouting, shouting, and shouting, for the very first time in his life.

And the congregation, surprised and pleased, let out with a chorus of "Amen's," for they knew what he now knew, that he was finally, truly, and totally in love.

Dee arrived at the landfill a few minutes before sunset. Incinerated trash of all kinds filled the rude ground cavities, while scattered heaps of fresh rubble waited to be burned. Inside the black plastic bag she lugged over her shoulder like a derelict Santa were all of the titles—*Hot Rod, Black and Huge, Dickalicious, Ruffneck Workout, Mo' Betta' Black Booty;* altogether more than two dozen DVDs and videos—the whole of the late Selma Fant's well worn treasure, including the illicit tapes of Brando and Collier.

The flames were immediate and aggressive, encouraged by a generous gasoline soaking. Coal-black smoke billowed in a twist toward the orange sky. She stood back and watched this part of Selma Fant's history disappear into the air, and she was both sad and glad. Selma had already lost so much, and drank herself to death out of guilt and unhappiness. An autopsy determined that she died of acute alcohol poisoning. It was time to let the soul of Selma Fant rest, finally, free of further scandal, scorn, and ridicule. After all, in spite of it all, in spite of the fact that she was a lonely old woman who drank herself to death, she was still the councilman's wife. That should count for something. Her only child cried over her passing. That should count for much. The time had come for Selma Fant to enjoy a dignity in death that she did not fully know in life.

Dee thought about her ex-husband, Kevin. She pulled out her cell phone and speed-dialed his number.

Epilogue

The Lucy Florence Coffeehouse is still going as strong as ever on Degnan Boulevard, as strong as the drums that beat in Leimert Park each and every Sunday afternoon. However, Brando and Omar have expanded their horizons, and they now freely act upon their culinary inquisitiveness. Their Sunday brunch ritual now explores the vast Southern California terrain—Malibu, Santa Monica, Marina Del Rey, Beverly Hills, Beachwood Canyon, Long Beach—where they explore a new and different eatery to surprise their Sabbath palate.

Still, Lucy Florence holds a very special place in their hearts, and they have decided that this Sunday will be their first Sunday back since Jeanette Bell's trial, since the death of Selma Fant, since what happened between them happened.

Brando sold his house on Don Pedro Drive—an inexplicable feeling of discomfort had replaced the serenity—and moved in with Omar. They are a committed couple now. Lovers. Friends and lovers. Partners in a monogamous relationship. From Omar, Brando learned to fully enjoy the passions of life. From Brando, Omar learned to channel his passions more productively.

Omar even goes to church these days, Brando's church, First AME, not because he has been struck with a sudden epiphany, but because this is where his man is on Sunday mornings. And maybe the stirring of the music has done it for him, the tambourines, the hand clapping, and the hugging. It all feels so good, maybe better, because there's a room full of people singing and clapping in harmonious happiness, carrying on like family.

Omar still has not reconciled with his mother, but all things in time.

Their lives are full now, Brando and Omar, and they are happy—grateful for the journey, the education, the stirring, and most of all, the love, a love no longer hidden but clear, visible, and free.

Vanessa Ellerbee can certainly see it from her booth in the corner at the coffeehouse where she and William have just brunched fillingly on the twins' Cajun omelet and sweet potato pie. She can see it as clear as day, the perfectly matched male couple stepping inside the door of Lucy Florence, greeted by a smiling wide-eyed twin, scolded for their absence, led to their regular table as if time had stood still.

Only half mad at them, Vanessa cannot help herself. She pats William gently on the hand and excuses herself. She gets up and makes her way over to the table where Brando and Omar have been seated.

"For awhile I thought you disappeared off the face of the earth." She pouts with a smile.

"Vanessa Ellerbee," Brando says slowly and warmly, standing to give her a hug. "How have you been?"

"Relieved now. You're alive."

"You remember Omar," Brando says.

"Yes, of course."

"Hello, Vanessa," Omar says, beginning to stand.

"Please. Don't get up," she protests gleefully.

"Don't worry. I'm going to the john," Omar continues knowingly. "Give you two a moment to catch up. Be right back, baby," he says to Brando. With loving eyes, Brando watches him cross the room.

"God, how long has it been?" Vanessa pulls his focus.

"Who knows?" he answers, gesturing her to the chair across from him. She sits.

"Actually since the little get-together at your place."

"But that didn't really happen, did it?" he reminds her.

"No it didn't."

"We missed Lucy Florence."

"Lucy Florence missed you."

"It's good to be back again. It's more appreciated."

"I thought you said he wasn't your lover." She smirks with a raised eyebrow.

"That was before we knew better." He smirks back.

"So what are we supposed to do now, handsome Bran? I mean, William and I?"

"I'm sure you'll find a way."

Slowly, seductively, she leans over and kisses him, holding his face gently in her hand. He smiles through the kiss, and then she does, too. Even slower than the kiss, she pulls back from him, to get a full view of his handsome face, so that he can get a full view of her beauty.

"The thrills you'll be missing," she says naughtily, "the thrills you almost had."

"I'm not sure they're thrills that I wanted."

"That's the problem. You're not sure."

"I'm as sure as anybody can be in life, Vanessa. That's the real thrill of it all. And I'm in love. That I'm sure of."

"Well," she huffs. "Listen, I should go. I think I'm in somebody's seat. It's been great seeing you again, Brando."

"Same here, Vanessa. Oh, and please give William my best."

"I will. He'll be glad you offered it."

She gets up and heads back toward her table; the stride in her step is sauntering; the church curls bounce ever so gently, in near slow motion. She arrives at her husband's questioning eyes.

She sits next to him and whispers in his ear. With his lobe at her lips he looks up slowly, across the room, at the table where Brando is studying the menu, where Brando's man rejoins him, where they smile at each other like two men in love.

The twins notice and slightly nod to each other. Drums begin faintly in the distance.

A whimsical sadness sparkles in William's eyes; in Vanessa's eyes, a fleeting regret, a smile that lives wounded but valiant on the fantasy of what could have been, what still could be, when fools, filled with desire, find a wee bit of hope to cling hopelessly to. After all, this is L.A., the city of angels, the city of infinite possibilities, where all one has to do is keep on . . . looking.

About the Author

Stanley Bennett Clay has received three NAACP Theatre awards for writing, directing, and coproducing the critically acclaimed play *Ritual*, as well as a Pan African Film Festival Jury Award for the film adaptation. The author of *Diva* and *In Search of Pretty Young Black Men*, he lives in Los Angeles.